HEART TRANSFORMED

The Potter's House Books - Book 13

KRISTEN M. FRASER

NOTE FROM THE AUTHOR

The 21 books that form **The Potter's House Books** series are linked by the theme of Hope, Redemption and Second Chances. They are all stand-alone books and can be read in any order. Books will become progressively available beginning March 27, 2018.

Book 1: The Homecoming by Juliette Duncan

Book 2: When it Rains by T.K. Chapin

Book 3: Heart Unbroken by Alexa Verde

Book 4: Long Way Home by Brenda S. Anderson

Book 5: Promises Renewed by Mary Manners

Book 6: A Vow Redeemed by Kristen M. Fraser

Book 7: Restoring Faith by Marion Ueckermann

Book 8: Unchained by Juliette Duncan

Book 9: Gracefully Broken by T.K. Chapin

Book 10: Heart Healed by Alexa Verde

Book 11: Place Called Home by Brenda S. Anderson

Book 12: Tragedy & Trust by Mary Manners

Book 13: Heart Transformed by Kristen M. Fraser

Books 14-21 to be advised.

Visit www.pottershousebooks.com for details of the latest release updates.

ALSO BY KRISTEN M. FRASER

The Whitecliffe Bay Series

Shining Grace

Holding Hope

Enduring Love

The Whitecliffe Bay Series Box Set

The Tallowood Valley Series

Heart on the Land

Bridge to Return

Home in the Valley

The Tallowood Valley Series Box Set

A Winter's Hope

The Potter's House Books

A Vow Redeemed

Heart Transformed

All of Kristen's books are available on Amazon.

Join Kristen's mailing list to receive sneak peeks, and find out about new releases and other deals. Sign up (http://www.kristenmfraser.com/newsletter-sign-up.html) - and receive *Lines of Promise* - free!

In my distress I prayed to the Lord,
and the Lord answered me
and set me free.
~Psalm 118: 5~

1

Coarse laughter sliced through the dank air. Genevieve eyed the pack of three women, much akin to prowling wolves, strolling around the perimeter of the drab, grey courtyard.

Shivering, she hunched her shoulders, bracing against the westerly wind biting through her thin green sweatshirt. Her heart hammered against her chest as the pack approached a lone woman pressed against the concrete wall. Scrawny with yellowing hair, the older woman drew her knees to her chest and gnawed on her fingernails, her eyes downcast as the trio leered at her, tossed a few ugly words her way and continued on their menacing walk.

Genevieve narrowed her eyes, watching their movements as they cussed at, or mocked anyone who dared look their way. Her back tensed. She'd fallen victim to their taunts before, and she didn't have the strength to face their insults today. The first few months within the grey walls of the Women's Correctional Centre had opened her eyes to an entirely different way of life, and had seen her develop a thicker skin, an armour to protect her emotions and self-esteem as a means to survive.

Karina Slater, her cell mate, had taken Genevieve under her wing, giving her guidance and tips for enduring her time in the women's prison. As a result, she'd learned who to talk to, and who to keep away from. And the women slowly approaching her were certainly ones to keep away from.

MOLLY ABBETS, THE SELF-IMPOSED RINGLEADER OF THE TRIO, WAS downright mean. Heartless and cruel would be better words to describe the solid-set woman with short-cropped black hair. Janet Niland and Susan Daintrey were fairly harmless by themselves, but Molly certainly called the shots when they were all together. Typical bullies, they were the dregs of society, now asserting themselves at the pinnacle of the prison hierarchy. Life behind the razor wire tended to be reverse of that in the outside world. The no-hopers were inclined to dominate, while the upper-crust of society were brought down a notch or two, toppled off their stilettos and tossed out of their McMansions up on Hamilton Hill, only to find themselves at the bottom of the pile.

At least that had been Genevieve's experience. Her fall from a life of privilege had been less than graceful, much to her parent's utter disgust and disdain. But when it came to the classes of society, she knew both sides of the coin. And it was the tail end, trusting the lies whispered against her skin that had landed her in the correctional facility exactly nine hundred and twelve days ago.

"WHATCHA DOIN' THERE, JIMMY?" A LOOSE PEBBLE SCUTTLED ACROSS the ground. Genevieve flinched at the nickname, an obvious barb to her flashy lifestyle before her Jimmy Choos were exchanged for the green Velcro-strapped running shoes now adorning her feet. She slowly raised her head, willing her pulse to slow. She would not show fear. She would not panic. She refused to let the women intimidate her.

"Drawing." Her eyes met Molly's piercing steel-grey ones. The other woman reached out, snatching the notebook out of Genevieve's hands. A sneer formed on her thin, cracked lips as she flicked through the worn pages. Genevieve swallowed. Only Karina and a few others had been privilege to the drawings within the spiral notebook. And her mother. She held her breath, waiting for the torment that always flowed from her mother's lips.

"Why are you wasting your time on that? Artists don't make any money. You're so much better than that." The harsh words tightened around her heart again. Along with echo of disappointment that always ensued. As an only child, Genevieve was expected to follow in her father's footsteps, pursuing a prestigious career in law. What a disappointment she'd been.

"This is good stuff, Jimmy." Janet's nasally voice broke through her thoughts. Her bony finger tapped on the open page as she glanced up from her position over Molly's right shoulder. Genevieve interlaced her fingers in the wire mesh fence behind her and shuffled her sneakers on the concrete.

"Thanks." Her sketches were of another time. Another life. Faded memories of what she'd left behind, and dreams of things yet to come. The ivory-coloured pages of her notebook were filled with sketches of the Brisbane River, the cliffs at Kangaroo Point, and the view from the jetty at New Farm Park. The pencil lines were crisp and clean, reminding her of the good times, before her choices led her into the prison cell she now occupied.

"Who's this?" Molly's callused finger poked at the face of an infant child. Pencil curls floated around the soft, angelic face staring back at her.

"No one," Genevieve murmured, smoothing her hand over her stomach as she glanced away. Even with daily exercise, loose skin remained, a bitter reminder of the selfish choices that had ruined her life.

"Hmph," Molly grunted and tossed the notebook into Genevieve's lap. Smoothing over the creased pages, Genevieve ran her fingers over the child's face as an alarm echoed around the courtyard, signalling time for the women to return to their cells for another evening. Pressing her lips together, an all-too familiar ache welled in her chest. Would the emptiness and torment of guilt ever leave her alone?

$\mathscr{H}$ 2 $\mathscr{H}$

"**G**reat effort today, guys." David Molineaux landed a friendly pat on each teen's back as they stepped down from the minivan. The motley group of boys ranged in age from mid to late teens with varying heights and stages of development to match.

Mumbled thanks, grunts and nods returned to David as the young men found their backpacks and ambled away towards their transport home.

The return trip to Brisbane from the three-day hike through the Lamington National Park had been rowdy to begin with. Friendly banter, typical of teenagers, filled the van as they made their way up the M1 towards the headquarters of Elevation Adventures, an outdoor adventure company based in Brisbane.

It was a completely different atmosphere to the first day of the hike, when there had been plenty of grumbling and cuss words floating around. By the second day, the boys had mellowed, and towards the final day, they didn't want to leave.

A glance in the rearview mirror as they entered suburbia brought a smile to David's face as he noted several pairs of drooping eyes, and heads swaying in time with the vehicle's movements. Despite some of the boys being quite challenging in their behaviour, the contented looks on their weary faces made it all worth the while.

The kids David took on hikes had already experienced far too much in their young lives. Life had dealt them a bad blow, and many had been in situations that no one of their age should find themselves in. He knew all too well what that was like. Which was why he'd reluctantly taken on the role as Program Coordinator for Elevation Adventures after going through the program himself as a troubled young adult. Reluctantly, because he didn't believe he was qualified to run such a program for at-risk teens. He was no saint.

"God doesn't call the qualified," Robert Simmons, the retiring director had said one evening as they sat on a bench seat outside the headquarters, overlooking the Brisbane River. "He qualifies the called. Of course, I can't take credit for those words, but it's true, nonetheless."

Somehow, Robert looked beyond David's past mistakes and saw the potential within. David had mumbled his way through Robert's affirmations, and somehow bumbled his way through the early days of his supposed calling. And now, after almost six years at the helm, he had never felt more alive.

DAVID GRABBED HIS BACKPACK FROM BEHIND THE DRIVER'S SEAT before closing and locking the door to the van.

"Thanks again, David." John Redmond strode over, his shoes crunching on the gravel in the parking lot. He grabbed David's hand in his own and gave a firm shake. The thick-set man, pushing sixty with tufts of white hair around his ears, was a chaplain at a youth centre just north of Brisbane. He worked alongside Elevation Adventures, sending at-risk youth on hikes to expose them to a positive environment and show them a different aspect of life than what they were used to.

"My pleasure." David shoved his hand into the pocket of his jeans and eyed the mish-mash of boys on the cusp of manhood as they climbed into the back of John's Land Cruiser. "They all seemed to enjoy themselves."

"That's great," John replied, stroking his chin. "It's always hard to know how things will go for them, but I've never heard anyone say a bad word yet."

"They never let on that they're having a good time. They're way too cool to show any enjoyment," David chuckled. "A few of them like to assert their position in the group on the first day, trying to act tough. But they usually all settle down after that."

"It's just not fair that they've got to go back to whatever awaits them at home." John shook his head, a flicker of sadness crossing his weathered features.

"It is a shame," David agreed, crossing his arms and leaning against the dust-caked panel of the minivan. The home life some of the kids endured made his stomach turn. "But you're making a difference. Don't ever forget that."

"As are you, my friend." John's thick hand clasped David's shoulder in a sign of solidarity and affirmation. "These outings and adventures that you take them on are experiences that will be carved into their memories forever. Regardless of what goes on behind closed doors, I know they'll have these good times to draw on when things get tough."

"I hope so," David murmured, eyeing the remaining boys lingering outside the office to be collected by their parents or guardians. He never liked this part – saying goodbye. Knowing that the kids would be returning to a less-than-favourable environment. One where they may not know where their next meal would be coming from. One full of neglect - or worse. His prayer, as small as it may be, was that he would somehow make a difference in their lives.

"Catch you next time." John gave David one last encouraging squeeze on his arm. David flung his backpack over his shoulder and watched the older man walk across the parking lot and hoist himself up into the dark green Land Cruiser.

"Have a good time, men?" John's voice boomed across the almost-vacant parking lot. The resounding whoops and yeses brought a smile to David's lips. He loved his job. Not that he'd call it a job. Getting to spend time outdoors, taking people hiking and exploring God's creation was hardly a chore. He especially loved sharing sunrises with the kids he took out, much to their protestations about getting up early. But they always changed their tune when they witnessed the dawning of a new day. It was almost a spiritual moment – as though God was giving His best to those who sacrificed sleep to watch the brilliant hues stretching out across the canvas of endless sky.

David hadn't missed a sunrise in the past five years. Except for cloudy or rainy days, he made a deal with himself not to miss the glorious moment God blessed the world with another new day. As each day dawned with its kaleidoscope of blues, oranges and pinks, he was reminded that the Lord's mercies are indeed new every morning. And he knew he would *never* take that gift for granted.

DUST SWIRLED IN THE AIR AS THE LAST OF THE CARS LEFT THE parking lot. David tossed his backpack onto the floor of his faded blue ute and slipped into the threadbare cloth-covered driver's seat. Weariness from the past few days washed over him as he turned the key in the ignition. The ute sputtered to life and he began the thirty-minute drive north along the M1 towards home. With a broken air-conditioning unit, he wound down the window, allowing the warm air from outside to circulate through the cab.

His thoughts turned to the weekend and the conversations he'd had with the young men while hiking through the rainforest. Once he'd proven he was trustworthy, many of them had opened up to him, giving him an insight into the struggles and challenges they faced on a daily basis. It broke his heart to hear their stories. Life wasn't fair, and through no fault of their own, hadn't always been kind to them. If only he could do more for them.

DAVID PULLED THE UTE TO A STOP IN THE DRIVEWAY OF HIS LOW-SET brick house. Set in a quiet street with established trees providing ample shade from the harsh afternoon sun, it was a far cry from his dream home. Built in the eighties, it still housed the original kitchen with its pine cabinetry, brown floor tiles and a dark green laminate bench top. He'd replaced the ghastly floral roller blind in the window above the sink with timber venetians, and had plans to replace the entire kitchen. One day. When time and finances allowed.

As he looped the keys over the hook behind the front door, David glimpsed his reflection in the mirror on the lounge room wall. What a sight! Given his appearance and the battered state of his much-loved vehicle parked in the driveway, anyone would think he lived rough. Three days hiking without any amenities would do that. His dark brown hair stood up at all angles. Dirt smeared his face. Even his neck appeared a darker colour.

His mattress beckoned as he tossed the backpack into his bedroom. What he would give to crawl into bed and sleep for days. As tempting as it was, the Sunday evening church service was his priority for now. Seeking first God's kingdom, no matter the sacrifice, was how he wanted to live his life. He was determined to give everything back to God, after He'd done so much for him.

After showering and washing the grime from the previous three days away, David changed into a clean pair of jeans and light grey long-sleeved shirt. Heading into the kitchen, he poured some dry cat food into a dish by the back door and topped up the matching water bowl.

"Not sure where you are this time, BC, but dinner's ready. I'm going out for a while. I might catch you later. Behave now." David shook his head and grinned to himself as he grabbed his jacket off the back of the dining chair. *Gosh, is that what happens when you live by yourself for too long? I'm seriously becoming a crazy cat man!*

3

The clunk of metal woke Genevieve. A prison guard grunted a greeting and slapped two trays onto the stainless steel bench on the opposite side of the small cell.

"Morning sunshine." Karina shifted on the plastic chair and grinned up at Genevieve.

"Morning." Genevieve blinked a few times and covered a yawn.

"Looks like we've got oat mash with a dash of milk this morning." Karina peered underneath one of the lids on the bowls. "Do you want yours up there?"

Genevieve stretched her arms above her head, relishing the sensation of her spine cracking. The top bunk mattress was nothing like she'd been used to in her own home, or the queen-sized one she'd shared with Ed. But at least she wasn't on the ground in a dark alley somewhere. She had that to be thankful for.

"I'll come down there." She took a moment to smooth her hair back into a ponytail before jumping down to the ground. Perching on the edge of the chair, she sat the plastic container of porridge on her lap.

"What's on your agenda today?" Karina asked between mouthfuls of her breakfast.

Genevieve chuckled, twirling the spoon between her fingers. "Oh, you know, a manicure. Then I might go and have a massage, do a spot of shopping before dinner and a movie with my hot date." She rolled her eyes and scooped the lukewarm goop into her mouth.

"Ah, that's the life." Karina's eyes sparkled as she leaned back against the chair. The women ate in comfortable silence, while the opening and closing of cell doors, and loud voices from guards and prisoners echoed along the corridor.

It was funny how life's circumstances had brought them together. Never in a million years would Genevieve have considered Karina a friend if she'd met her outside prison. She wouldn't have glanced twice at the older woman with the short salt and pepper hair if they'd passed each other on the street. Karina grew up in the poorer suburbs, and ran with the wrong crowd from an early age. Genevieve had grown up with everything given to her, yet threw it all away. In her world, money and status were everything. Or so she was led to believe. All she'd ever wanted to hear from her parents were, "*We love you*", "*We're proud of you*." Instead, "*Not good enough*", "*Work harder*", and "*Don't do anything to bring shame upon our family name*" were constantly tossed at her by her aloof and overbearing parents. Her father was too occupied with his legal practice, while her mother was too busy keeping an immaculate house and hanging off her father's arm at all the prestigious events in the city to offer their love. All Genevieve wanted was acceptance. And love. Which was why she'd fallen so easily into the arms of charming Edward Macintosh.

"ARE YOU THERE, GEN?" KARINA SNAPPED HER FINGERS. LOWERING her eyes, Genevieve offered a small smile.

"Sorry. Just thinking."

"Don't let your thoughts bring you down, sweetheart." Karina's gentle words wrapped around her heart. She'd never known concern or compassion like that. But what a way to earn it. A three year jail term. Disowned by her family. An almost-finished law degree she would never be able to complete. And the thing that grieved her the most, the one thing she'd never shared with anyone other than Ed – the loss of an innocent child.

"Each day is a new one. If you dwell on the past, you'll stay there. If you think too far ahead, you'll be consumed by worry. Just face today and whatever it may bring."

Genevieve nodded, scraping her spoon across the bottom of the bowl. Karina was right. There was no point worrying about what lay ahead. Nor was there any point worrying about the path her life had taken. The damage had been done. She could only learn from her mistakes and move forward.

"You're too kind, Karina." Genevieve placed her unfinished porridge on the tray and slid it against the wall.

"It's the only way to be, love." Kindness. Had she ever known true kindness? As her life spiralled out of control, she had never been one to demonstrate kindness. In fact, her choices had been purely selfish, and made out of fear and the longing to be accepted, not to be kind.

Genevieve stood and crossed the room to the bunk beds. Standing on the bottom bunk, she pulled the top sheet and blanket up over her mattress.

"You can shower first."

"Are you sure?" Genevieve glanced over her shoulder as she fluffed up the pillow. Stepping down off the lower bunk, she grabbed clean underwear and a fresh tracksuit of the shelf. Taking a breath, she moved behind the half wall where the lidless stainless steel toilet bowl leered at her. She stripped off and stepped into the stained concrete shower. Gone were the days of luxurious showers using a loofah and whatever expensive shower gel took her fancy. Now it was a quick wash using a prison-issued flannel and a small cake of soap. Her toes curled with the awful sensation of wet concrete beneath her feet as she quickly washed. After drying, she shimmied into the green tracksuit she'd become accustomed to wearing.

"Your turn." Running a brush through her hair, she twisted it into a plait.

As Karina showered, Genevieve pulled out her notebook and sat at the bench. There were a few minutes before they would leave the cell and their day would truly begin. For now, she would focus her thoughts on the pencil strokes on her page. Dark. Light. Shadows. It was one thing that kept her sane. One thing she knew she was good at, despite her mother's negative words vying for space in her head.

"You should sell them." Karina walked over to the bench, running the thin towel over her damp hair.

"Right." A short laugh erupted from Genevieve as she circled an arm around the page, shielding her work from Karina.

"What? You should." Karina tossed the towel into the linen bag in the corner of the cell. "You're very good at capturing depth and emotion."

Genevieve turned on the chair." And may I ask who would buy drawings done by a prisoner? It's not exactly a selling point."

"You'd be surprised." Karina nodded her head knowingly as she sat on the edge of the bed and slid on her sneakers.

"Well, I can't imagine anyone I know wanting anything. Gosh, imagine the controversy!" She chuckled, envisaging how horrified her parents and their acquaintances would be if they discovered their artwork had been created in jail.

"The prison has links with some galleries on the outside. Some of the indigenous population have their work displayed and sold there."

Would people really pay for her work?

"Do you really think they're good?" She asked, flicking through the pages of her notebook.

"I wouldn't say anything if I didn't mean it," Karina replied.

"Thanks," Genevieve murmured, embracing the small thrill of possibility that something good could come of her imprisonment.

4

Fluorescent lights flickered overhead as Genevieve shuffled along the corridor behind other women making their way to their prison jobs. Inmates, unless medically unfit, were expected to work while serving their sentence. Some worked in the laundry. Others worked in the kitchen. Women also worked in the vegetable gardens within the prison grounds, sowing and harvesting fresh produce for the kitchen to use in their meals.

Genevieve made her way through the airlock and out of the building, following the concrete path bathed in sunlight. Karina had already gone to her job of sorting and packaging headphones for the airlines.

Genevieve and four other women entered a building set away from the main one. Never in her wildest dreams had she imagined she would train as a hairdresser. But here she was, strapping on a black apron and setting up a portable trolley, ready for the morning ahead.

A small group of women sat along the chairs in the front of the prison salon, flicking through the latest gossip magazines. To the outside world, the salon rivalled that of any found in a shopping mall. Posters of models with the latest hairstyles adorned the walls. Music played from the stereo. The sound of hairdryers and constant chatter filled the air. A chalkboard displayed a menu of styles and prices.

A younger woman with blonde hair and dark roots took a seat in the black vinyl chair in front of Genevieve.

"Good morning, Katy. What are we doing today?" She ran her hair through the woman's shoulder-length locks.

"Just neatening it up. I've got my hearing soon, and would like to be a little more presentable."

"Oh, I hope it goes well for you." Genevieve caught Katy's eye in the mirror. She'd already been in the system for three years for drug possession and burglary, and was coming up for another parole hearing. "Do you want me to touch up the roots today?"

"Nah. Just a cut and maybe style it a bit. Gotta make a good impression, hey."

Genevieve smiled. Katy looked much older than her twenty-three years. The harsh choices she'd made had aged her early. Genevieve's shoes squeaked on the linoleum floor as she moved behind the other woman. Who was she to judge? She'd made wrong choices too. And now with a few weeks remaining of her own sentence, she was determined to put all that behind her and focus on the future.

Draping a black plastic cape over Katy, she fastened it at her nape before leading her over to one of the sinks. Turning the taps on, she flicked her wrist under the running water, adjusting the flow until she was satisfied with the temperature.

"Mmm, that feels good." Katy smiled, her eyes closed as Genevieve lathered shampoo through her hair and massaged her scalp. She rinsed, conditioned and rinsed again. After wrapping a towel around Katy's head, the two women made their way back to Genevieve's work station.

"Will you have support at your hearing?" Genevieve ran the comb through Katy's wet hair. Pulling some clips out of her apron, she pinned strands of hair on top of her head.

Katy shrugged. "I'm not sure. My brother's pretty busy." Her eyes flickered down and she jiggled her foot back and forth.

"Well, I hope someone's there for you." Genevieve recalled the stony silence and solemn faces of her parents when they fronted court for her sentencing. The permanent scowl on her mother's lips, even more tightly pinched, and the cold detachment from her father that could be felt across the courtroom, magnified her sense of isolation. By then, she'd already lost her friends. And all her father's money, prestige and law associates weren't enough to save her from prison. Funny how people distance themselves when one breaks the law.

"Yeah, me too. Dave's always been my supporter. I don't know why, especially as everyone else ditched me."

"I know what that's like," Genevieve mused, strands of dark blonde hair falling to the floor as she snipped and styled Katy's hair. "He sounds like a good brother."

"Yeah, he is," Katy whispered. The hard edges of her face softened as she ran her fingers over the hem of the cape draped over her shoulders.

Genevieve began blow-drying Katy's hair before holding a mirror up to the back and catching Katy's eyes.

Katy turned her head from side-to-side, taking in her new hairstyle. "Awesome. Thanks, Gen. You're so good at this."

A sense of satisfaction bubbled up and brought a smile to Genevieve's lips as she removed the cape from Katy. Genuine compliments, without any hint of vested interest, were foreign to her. It didn't make sense that complete strangers, with no reason to offer praise, were able to compliment her, while her parents could only manage criticism at best.

"I really hope everything goes well for you."

"Thanks. Me too. But if it doesn't, it's only another two years." Katy tossed her new do over her shoulders and gave a self-deprecating laugh. "What's another two years of my life in here?"

Katy ambled over to the counter, reached into her pocket and slapped payment for her haircut onto the bench. Genevieve swept the discarded hair into a pile before attending to another client. The morning flew by. The constant chatter of women, the low hum of hair-dryers, and the beat of the music made the salon a fun place to be.

Genevieve smiled to herself as she tidied her station at the end of the work day. It surprised her how much she enjoyed working in the salon. And how much the tables had turned. Her parents would be appalled to discover their daughter, the one whom they'd desired to have a successful law career, would be a qualified hairdresser by the time her prison sentence was finished.

5

After rising early Tuesday morning to witness yet another glorious sunrise from his back porch, David showered, tossed a sandwich and an apple into his backpack, and headed into the office of Elevation Adventures.

The headquarters were housed in a converted shipping container on a quiet leafy bend of the Brisbane River. Brett Rainville, Libby Danbrook and Simon Walburn worked alongside him as instructors and tour guides.

Despite the early hour, the river was already alive with activity. Rowers in sleek boats skimmed across the glistening surface of the river as David pulled his ute into the parking lot. The red *City-Hopper* zig-zagged across the brown ribbon of water, ferrying people to their various stops along the river.

David was always the first one to arrive at work. Partly because he loved his job. And partly because being alone for too long at home didn't sit well with him. He needed to keep busy. Left alone with his thoughts for too long would send him spiralling into his past. Although he'd fully recovered from his narcotics addiction, and had been clean for five years, the guilt and shame lay just beneath the surface, ready to break through and cripple him at any given moment.

After deactivating the building's security alarm, David flicked the air conditioning on. Tossing his backpack underneath his desk, he logged onto his computer and strode over to the whiteboard, perusing the list of outings that were booked for the coming weeks. Another hike at the end of the week with a different group of teens. A corporate high-ropes challenge he would assist Brett with. Some rock climbing at Kangaroo Point Cliffs. And a few day tours, kayaking along the river.

David printed off the day's schedule, placing a copy on each of his colleague's desks, before making a cup of coffee in the small kitchenette at the back of the office. The kitchenette consisted of nothing more than a sink, one cupboard and enough room to make a sandwich on the countertop, and overlooked a slightly overgrown stretch of grass which the team took turns mowing. To the left was a storage shed for the kayaks, paddleboards, oars and other equipment required for the business. To the right, if you leaned far enough forward with your face almost pressed against the glass, you could just make out the steel arch of the Story Bridge.

David slid open the glass door and stepped outside with his steaming coffee. Rays of sunlight streamed through the cluster of trees on the opposite side of the parking lot. Silver sequins danced across the water lapping quietly on the shore. This was another reason he enjoyed arriving early. The quiet of the morning, the beauty of the water and the light breeze rustling through the treetops calmed his soul before the busyness of the day took hold.

Sipping his coffee, David turned his face towards the warmth of the sun. *Thank you, Lord, for this amazing day you've gifted me. Please go before me and lead my steps. And may all I do bring glory to your name.*

The rest of the team soon arrived, David's lone minutes of quiet dissolving with his last drop of coffee. Soon after nine, the first participants for the morning's kayak tour arrived. Eight people in total. A mix of young and old. Couples and singles. Men and women. By half-past, they'd assembled on a clearing on the riverbank just a few metres down from the headquarters, and David led them through the obligatory safety routine and instructions before pairing everyone up and assigning them a kayak.

With life jackets fastened, and oars in hand, the group waded out into the shallows of the river. Loud splashing and squeals of laughter rang out as two of the younger women slipped while attempting to climb into their kayak. David chuckled. It always happened.

"We're not here for a swim, ladies!" Brett grinned as he waded over and stilled their craft. After much laughter and more splashing, the women were seated and ready for their exploration of the river. Brett led the group away from the shallows of the bank, while David and his companion brought up the rear.

A cloudless blue sky provided the backdrop for a perfect morning on the river. The group passed the Kangaroo Point Cliffs and the Maritime Museum. A ferry chugged past, leaving the kayaks bobbing up and down in its wake.

"All good, everyone?" Brett angled his craft to face the group.

A chorus of affirmation rang out and the group continued. At the halfway point, they guided the kayaks into a quiet section of the river and pulled them into the sandy shore. Brett and David unpacked morning tea consisting of a fruit platter, choc-chip cookies and brie cheese with crackers. Both men mingled with the guests, getting to know a little about them. Many of the people who booked in for an adventure had never attempted kayaking before, and it always gave David great joy to see them overcome their trepidation and embrace the experience.

"This is fantastic." A man, David guessed to be in his mid-fifties, settled onto the soft sand next to David. "You're lucky to have such a great job."

Taking a swig of water from his bottle, David nodded and grinned. "Yeah, it's pretty good."

"I'm Tom Matterson." He wiped his hand on the leg of his grey cargo shorts and shook David's hand.

"David."

"How long have you been doing this for?" Tom removed his sunglasses and looped them over the neck of his shirt, his green eyes surveying their surroundings.

David looped his fingers over his knees and gazed out across the river, now alive with activity. "Going on six years now. Have you kayaked before?"

"Oh, many moons ago. My wife gave me a voucher for my birthday. She thinks I'm stuck behind my desk too much at work and have become sedentary in my old age. She's right, of course." Tom's laugh bellowed out around the inlet, and a few members of the group turned around to see what the fuss was about.

"Kind of like a mid-life crisis thing?" David chuckled.

"Cheaper than a Harley." Tom exploded with laughter again and David couldn't help but be caught up with his infectious laugh. "I used to spend a lot of time on the water when I was younger, but time and work got the better of me. Which seems to be the case of everyone these days. I didn't realize how much I missed the freedom of being on the water." Tom adjusted his maroon cap, embroidered with the symbol of the state's favourite football team, and gazed wistfully at the water.

"It's great, isn't it?" David tilted his neck upwards, enjoying the serenity of the secluded cove. The distant hum of cars on the M1 carried down from the overpass. Water lapped rhythmically on the muddy shore and golden shards of sunlight filtered through the branches of the weeping willows at the water's edge. The sheltered bend in the river was heaven amid the chaos of the daily hustle and bustle of the city.

"How'd you get into this anyway? I mean, how does someone land a job taking people out on the water?"

David puffed his cheeks up as he blew out a breath. His heart hammered against his chest. It was a question he always hoped to avoid. His colleagues knew some of the details of his past. But he wasn't in the practice of divulging his drug addiction to strangers, particularly those who'd paid for a premium adventure. He didn't want to taint their experience, nor did he want to tarnish the reputation that Robert had worked so hard to build. David wasn't the same man he was all those years ago. But he knew how fickle and unforgiving people could be. Not everyone understood grace.

"A friend offered me the position, and I accepted." He gave a slight shrug. That was part of the truth.

"Did you have any prior experience? Or did you just learn on the job?" Tom turned towards David, genuine interest displayed on his face. Frowning behind the security of his sunglasses, David glanced across at the other guests. Laughter floated across the sandy patch, and Brett's voice rose above the low murmur of conversation as he shared humorous anecdotes of previous adventures. Why couldn't Tom leave him alone and go join the others? He shook his head. He shouldn't be irritated. Tom seemed a nice guy, and genuinely interested in what David's job entailed. It wasn't his fault David had a past he'd rather keep hidden.

"I ..." David cleared his throat. Plucking a pebble out of the sand, he rolled the smooth stone between his fingers, willing his heart to slow. *Not now, Lord. Please not now. Why on earth would this guy need to hear my story?*

David drew his arm back and cast the rock into the water, watching as it skipped across the surface a few times before it sank.

"I learned most of it on the job." He drew one knee to his chest and expelled his breath. "We run programs for disadvantaged youth. I went on one of the hikes when I was a young adult, which is how I met Robert, the previous owner." He cast a glance at Tom, waiting for him to recoil in shock.

"Huh. That's interesting." Tom pursed his lips and nodded.

"What is?" *The fact that I'm not some clean-cut guy with an education higher than high school? The fact that I was a wayward teen?*

"I run a prison outreach through our local church. My wife Tricia and I visit the prisons, establish a relationship with the prisoners, and also offer support on their release. I wonder ..." The older man's voice trailed off as he shifted into a more comfortable position on the sand.

"Time to get going, team." Brett's booming voice sounded across the clearing. "Pop your rubbish in here. Thanks." Brett nodded as members of the group placed their discarded scraps in the plastic bag he held open, before dragging their kayaks back into the water. David inwardly sighed, grateful for Brett's interruption. Tom pushed himself off the ground, dusted his pants off and took a moment to stretch his back. "Don't get old mate. This body creaks and groans all the time."

David chuckled as he stood and brushed off his pants. "Don't worry. Mine's doing it too."

"Can I have a chat with you when we get back to your office?" Tom queried as they dragged the kayaks into knee-deep water.

"Sure thing," David replied over his shoulder. The return trip up the river would give him some time to think over their conversation. Tom's words piqued his interest, but also made him uncomfortable.

The procession of kayaks ventured back up the river, with Brett playing tour guide out the front.

"Twenty-three ferry terminals were damaged in the Brisbane floods. The river broke its banks and floodwater inundated the city." Murmurs rose up from the group. David recalled the floods, and how some of the motorway went under; many properties were damaged, including their own at Elevation Adventures. But now as he rowed on the water, surrounded by the sights and sounds of the bustling city, it seemed hard to believe the floods had even occurred.

Water flicked up on his legs as he settled into the rhythm of rowing. He loved the open water. Brisbane was a beautiful city. Unfortunately, he also knew most of the dark alleys of the city all too well. But he was forever thankful for his newfound freedom to enjoy everything the city had to offer.

❧ 6 ❧

Libby greeted the group with cool drinks set on a table in the shade of a large Moreton Bay fig tree.

While the group stood around conversing, David draped the life jackets over a railing at the end of the parking lot. The bright orange of the vests contrasted with the muted green grass.

"Have you got a moment, David?" Tom approached with a white plastic cup in his hand. David hung the last jacket over the rail, flicking the plastic clasps of the safety belt to the side. Turning, to face the other man, he wiped his hands on his shorts.

"Sure." He leaned against the railing and tucked his hands into his pockets.

"This is a great business you've got here." Tom swept his hand around.

"Thanks. We all enjoy doing it, and it seems everyone enjoys what we do. I guess it's a win-win for everyone."

Tom pressed his lips together, looking into his cup as he swirled the liquid around. "So, I mentioned earlier that my wife and I were involved in prison ministry."

David nodded slowly, eyeing the older man. His navy blue polo shirt pulled taut across his shoulders. Tufts of sandy hair poked out from underneath his cap. Lines of time faintly feathered his tanned skin.

"You mentioned working with at-risk teens. I'm wondering if you would be interested in working with prisoners?" Tom tilted his chin, his eyes focused on David. Thankful for his sunglasses, David averted his gaze as a myriad of thoughts passed through his mind. *Prisoners? That's a huge leap from teenagers.*

"I know it's a big ask, and probably seems quite daunting."

"No, no. Not at all." David shook his head and lifted his gaze to meet Tom's. "Well, maybe a little." He chuckled, scuffing his water shoes across a patch of an almost-bare patch of grass. His thoughts turned to his younger sister Kaitlin, serving time for burglary and drug possession. Gosh, they were a messed up pair.

A smile tugged at his lips as he imagined kayaking up the river with her. Her blonde hair floating around her face. Her infectious laugh bubbling through the air. She would love it. She'd always been the adventurous type. His smile quickly faded as he thought ahead to her parole hearing and the fact he wouldn't be there. Would she even be granted parole? Would she be able to enjoy the freedom he had?

"... offenders from maximum security ..."

David's head flicked up at Tom's words. "Sorry, Tom. What were you saying?"

Tom took a sip from his cup and wiped his mouth on the back of his hand. "Just that the groups would be those on parole, or those who have been fully released. So there's no need to worry about offenders from maximum security mixing with the public."

Stroking his chin, David gazed around the parking lot where a few remaining clients lingered. Libby and Simon were down by the water's edge, preparing the kayaks for another outing. "It sounds interesting." Prisoners weren't a foreign concept to him, having visited Kaitlin numerous times at the Women's Correctional Centre. But visiting in a secure environment, with prison guards watching your back, was completely different to inviting them onto his own turf.

TOM LEANED AGAINST THE RAILING NEXT TO DAVID AND FOLDED HIS

arms. "I think it would be a great opportunity for them. Give them something to look forward to, and help boost their self-esteem. I'm sure many of them would never have experienced anything like what you offer here. Many of them have had rough upbringings, so opportunities like this would never have presented themselves."

David mulled over Tom's words as two cars drove out of the parking lot. He glanced at his watch. There was just over an hour before the next group would arrive for their abseiling adventure at Kangaroo Point Cliffs.

At least his job was never boring. And he loved watching people overcome their fears and conquer new horizons. *Would it be so bad to extend the same opportunity to prisoners? Prisoners?! I just don't know.*

Tom tipped his cup back, draining the last drops of water into his mouth.

"Leave it with me, Tom. I'll have a chat with the others and get back to you."

AFTER EXCHANGING CONTACT DETAILS IN THE OFFICE, DAVID leaned back in his chair and drummed his fingers on the desk. Could Tom's proposal work?

"Just popping out to grab some lunch. Can I get you anything?" Brett poked his head around the front door.

"Nah, I'm good thanks," David replied. His sandwich and apple would be enough for the day. Rarely did he spend money on takeaway food. Preparing nourishing foods for a healthy lifestyle had been part of his rehabilitation, and it stopped him from replacing one addiction with another.

"No worries. I'll be back soon and give you a hand with this afternoon's climb." Brett tapped his fingers on the wall in a farewell salute.

With Libby and Simon outside, the quiet of the office gave David time to contemplate Tom's proposition. It both excited and scared him. Sure, he was used to working with troubled teens – getting alongside them and being a positive role model in the hope they would see there was more to life than the lure of drugs and alcohol. It certainly wasn't easy, with many of the kids carrying so much anger and defiance from their home life. But, could they open Elevation Adventures up to ex-offenders? How much harder would it be working with ex-cons? What would the general public think of that? Would it scare business away once people knew?

Someone gave me a chance to turn my life around, and I am forever grateful. The least I can do is extend that opportunity to others. Oh, Lord, show me what you would have me do.

7

A high-pitched alarm rang out through the prison compound. Prison guards in the hair salon jumped to action, pacing around the room and speaking into their two-ways. Silence, apart from the piercing sound of the alarm, descended across the room as hairdryers were switched off. *A lockdown.* Genevieve returned the appliance to her station and watched, her heart pounding in her chest.

She'd never experienced a lockdown during her incarceration, but Karina had told her about previous ones. A brawl between different prison gangs. An assault on a prison guard. A prisoner self-harming.

Genevieve glanced around at the handful of women in the salon. Helen, her trainer, stood by the front counter. Marion and Sammy, two other trainees, stood near the sinks. Jodie and Natalie, who both worked in the prison laundry, were seated in chairs awaiting their cut and colour.

"Okay, ladies. You know the drill." The younger, stocky prison guard strode to the middle of the salon, while the other guard marched around the internal perimeter, ensuring all entry and exit points were secure.

"What do you reckon's goin' on?" Jodie swung around in her chair, the black cape dwarfing her gaunt frame.

"Dunno," Natalie replied from a nearby chair, her wet hair clinging to her head.

Genevieve's heart pounded in her chest. The plastic tray of her work station cut into her palms as her grip tightened on the trolley.

"It's alright, darl." Marion swept cuttings of hair into a pile. "It's probably nothing too bad. We're safe here anyway."

"Are you sure?" Genevieve glanced around at the guards pacing around the room. Every so often, they would peer out the windows and speak into the two-ways attached to their lapels.

"Everyone's good in here, aren't we?" Jodie called out to the other women. Rough laughter, from smoking-affected larynxes, erupted around the room. Genevieve swallowed the bile forcing its way up her throat as she eyed the scissors on the bench. How easy would it be for someone to grab them and cause harm? A shiver ran through her at the thought. She knew she rubbed shoulders with the likes of arsonists, thieves and other addicts. But had any of them harmed someone with a weapon?

The taller prison guard caught her eye and gave a slight nod of his head. Was it a sign of reassurance? Or was it confirmation of her fears? Tears sprang in her eyes. She couldn't wait for her sentence to be over to escape the constant fear of something going wrong.

Turning her back on the other women, she busied herself tidying her trolley. She straightened the hair clips and placed the combs together. Folding a towel, she blinked away the tears. She wouldn't let anyone see her cry. She didn't want to be weak. She didn't want word getting out that she was soft; the spoilt rich kid gone bad, unable to cope with prison life. It might be true, but she didn't need reminding of how stupid and reckless she'd been.

"You alright, hun?" A warm hand rested on her shoulder. Helen's husky voice broke through her thoughts. Genevieve pressed her lips together and nodded. Wiping her eyes on the sleeve of her shirt, she turned and faced the other woman. "I'm okay," she whispered. How could the other women remain so calm with the incessant alarm signifying something was not right? The unknown terrified her, but she wasn't going to admit she was afraid.

"We're safe here." Helen gently squeezed her arm and perched on the backless stool behind the counter. "No-one's coming in or going out."

"How long will we be in lockdown for?"

"Not sure, love. Sometimes it's a couple of hours. Sometimes a whole day. It depends on the situation. We may be able to move out later, depending on what's going on." Helen nodded towards the prison guards standing in front of the door.

"Gosh, I hope we're not here all day. Not that I don't think you're great." She forced a smile at the other woman. Helen's short spiky hair matched the purple shade of her shellac nails. Earrings of various shapes and sizes pierced her ears, and she wore an array of thin gold chains around her neck. Her image, combined with her throaty voice, screamed, *'lower class citizen'.* Genevieve would never have looked twice at her outside the razor wire fence. But this woman was one of her closest friends. Had she really been such a snob – judging people by their appearance and labels of their clothing? It pained her to know she had lived such a shallow, meaningless life. And it was moments like this that gave Genevieve a reality check, reminding her once again of how far she'd fallen.

"Well, we may as well make the most of it," Helen announced. "Who's up for a manicure?"

"I'll have one." Natalie waved her hands in the air. A resounding chorus went up from the other women.

Genevieve finished drying Jodie's hair, while Helen poured cups of water for everyone. With the faint strains of music playing on the stereo, Marion and Sammy set up the manicure station.

Conversation and laughter drifted around the room. And gossip about visitors, court appearances and exes – which Genevieve was more than happy to contribute to – soon occupied their time. Genevieve couldn't help but smile. It was a strange concept to consider these women as her friends.

🙦 8 🙤

By the time they were released from the lockdown, Genevieve's stomach was growling. Two boxes of uneaten sandwiches, and two cartons of milk sat on the bench in her cell. Frowning, Genevieve cast a quick glance around the empty room. Both beds were made. Everything was in its right place. The cell was just as they'd left it that morning.

She opened one of the sandwich boxes and took a bite, the dry bread sticking to the roof of her mouth. Slurping milk from the carton to wash the tasteless meat and cheese down, she waited. Where was Karina?

Sunlight filtered through the frosted-glass windows onto the cell floor. The lockdown meant there was no outdoor time, and the women were confined to their cells for the remainder of the day.

Genevieve pulled her notebook off the shelf. Tracing her fingers over the drawings, Genevieve recalled Karina's words of encouragement to sell her work. Was it possible? Maybe she could teach art classes once her sentence was complete. Perhaps she could offer work for commission. *Really, Gen? Who are you kidding? People won't buy your work, because you will always be tainted by this. You will never escape the fact that you've been in prison.*

Genevieve shifted on the cold plastic chair, its legs slightly buckling as it moved on the ground. Straightening her back, she gripped the pencil and continued sketching. Her thoughts and emotions flowing through her fingers as she added shading to the paper.

"Trehearn." A guard rapped on the window of her cell before the door opened.

Genevieve snapped to attention, her hands immediately covering her work as they always did when someone was near. Her heart hammered in her chest. Was it a cell search? Had she done something wrong? She tried to recall anything that might be considered a violation. She came up empty. Keeping mostly to herself and the few women she trusted ensured she followed every rule within the prison walls. Had someone set her up – or planted contraband in the cell?

"Slater's been taken to hospital." The guard's deep voice bounced off the cell walls. He stood tall in the doorway, his hands crossed in front of him.

"What?" The pencil dropped out of her hand and clattered to the floor. "What happened? What's wrong with her?" Pressing her hands together in her lap, Genevieve nervously eyed the baton and can of capsicum spray fastened to the guard's belt.

"Hurt during a ruckus that caused the lockdown. She received some heavy knocks and was KO'd. She's been taken to hospital to get checked out." Voices echoed through the corridor outside the cell. *Karina was injured?* How could she be involved in the brawl? That wasn't like her at all.

"Can you tell me anything else?" Genevieve steadied her voice as she locked eyes with the guard.

"Sorry." The collar on his shirt puckered as he shook his head. Genevieve glanced down at her tightly wound fingers. As much as she didn't like being in a prison cell, Karina made it bearable and she always felt safe with her around.

Without another word, the guard turned and pulled the door closed behind him. The four walls pressed in on Genevieve, and tears welled in her eyes as she contemplated being without her cell mate.

Karina had been her saving grace when she first entered the correctional centre. How would she cope without her? The noises echoing through the corridors at night - the moans, the wailing, the banging - filled her with dread.

She leaned down and picked up the pencil. Sucking in her bottom lip, she turned to a new page in the notebook and began sketching. Thick, dark lines filled the page as she poured out her fear and angst at the prospect of being alone.

9

David ran a hand over his face and straightened the collar on his charcoal grey button-up shirt. He'd paired it with blue jeans and black slip-ons, making it easy to remove for the security search. Visitation days always made him nervous. The fifty minute drive to Wacol brought back memories of his own transgressions, and how easily it could have been him behind bars.

Another few hours west, and he'd arrive in the small town where all his and Kaitlin's problems began.

It had been a nothing town back then, and was even worse now, with many shops closing down and businesses going bust.

His mother still lived on the acreage they'd grown up on, and he wasn't sure who her current beau was. David recalled the countless parties hosted in the paddock. The bonfires with their flames licking the dark sky. The creek flowing through the property, bordered by river gums, provided the perfect setting for nights fuelled by alcohol and drugs.

His mother, Dorothy, or "Dot", as she liked to be known, always turned a blind eye to the goings-on in the paddock. *"As long as I don't see it, I don't care what you do."*

David's friends thought it was fantastic that he had such a relaxed mother. But she was always too busy chasing after wealthy farmers or other men at the town dances to care for anyone beside herself. There'd been at least four different men in the family home since his father passed away. Dot was always too concerned with her own needs to bother nurturing her relationship with David and Kaitlin.

Perhaps if she had paid more attention, then Kaitlin wouldn't be in prison with a four-year sentence to her name. Perhaps if he'd been more vigilant as an older brother, Kaitlin wouldn't have followed in his footsteps.

He cringed with the memory of finding Kaitlin unconscious after a wild night of partying together. At the time, he thought it had been a great night of sibling bonding – sharing shots and passing around joints. As those images replayed in his mind, it filled him with incredible sadness that he'd been so stupid to ruin his sister's life.

David see-sawed between anger and regret as he left the M1, driving past the used car sales yards, past the fish-and-chip shop and other dilapidated buildings that had seen better days. Towering eucalypts bordered the stretch of road leading to the correctional centre. Signs warning motorists they were entering prison territory appeared on the roadside. And soon, the familiar sight of razor wire fencing emerged through the clearing of trees.

David turned his head to the open window, sucking in a lungful of fresh air in an attempt to calm his nerves. His palms were sweaty as they gripped the steering wheel.

There were only a few cars in the parking lot as David pulled to a stop a short walk from the main entrance. Adjusting the collar of his shirt, and buttoning his sleeves at the wrist, he stepped out of the ute and closed the door. He took a moment to size up the prison. He could see movement beyond the fence as prisoners went about their day. He'd been here numerous times since Kaitlin's incarceration, and yet it still filled him with trepidation.

AFTER CHECKING THROUGH THE SECURITY POINT, DAVID JOINED A small group of visitors and followed a prison officer to the official visiting area. The group – an older couple, a young woman with a little

34

boy, a heavily tattooed man who towered over everyone else, and David – made a solemn procession winding through the empty corridors until they arrived at some double doors.

The officer ushered them through to a room with numerous tables and chairs set up. Fluorescent lights bathed the room in a dull glow, highlighting the peeling paint on the walls. Prison officers stood guard around the simple room. Their eyes scrutinized each visitor, and burned a hole into David's back as he walked over to the table where his sister waited.

A grin broke on Kaitlin's face as he approached, and David couldn't help but return her smile. His shoulders relaxed, and the angst he'd felt on the drive dissipated as they embraced – the one time they were allowed to hug. He held Kaitlin tight, treasuring the moment with her, and silently pouring out his remorse into his embrace.

"You look good, Katy." They sat down on plastic chairs on opposite sides of the metal table. Kaitlin's blonde hair hung in loose waves around her face. Her green eyes were bright, her skin clear. And she'd even put on a little weight. Not that he'd mention that part. No woman wants to hear she's put on weight.

"Thanks. As do you." Her grin revealed stained and crooked teeth. Something he would help her fix on her release, if she wanted.

"Sorry I haven't updated my wardrobe since last time you were here." Kaitlin gestured to her prison greens. A chuckle escaped David and he shook his head. "Funny girl." He was proud of the changes he'd seen in her. It was a shame a prison sentence had been the catalyst.

"So, big brother." Kaitlin leaned back on the chair and folded her arms. "What's been happening with you? I haven't seen you for awhile."

"Yeah, sorry I haven't been in sooner," he mumbled, running a hand across his jaw. "And sorry I couldn't make it to your hearing." Guilt twisted in his gut at the brief flicker of hurt in her eyes.

"I am truly sorry, Katy." He leaned forward, folding his hands on the table, the metal cool beneath his arms. "I ..." His gaze tracked to the window behind her right shoulder. Branches moved up and down in the breeze, taunting prisoners with their freedom of movement.

"You don't need to apologize, David. It's okay." Kaitlin sniffed, tilting her chin. "I don't expect you to drop everything to come and hang out with your sister in jail." A self-deprecating laugh escaped her lips.

"I *do* want to see you." David frowned. Of course he wanted to. He thought of her every day. It was hard not to, when guilt plagued him relentlessly. Admittedly, work consumed a lot of his time, and he hadn't been to see her as much as he would've liked.

"Dave, you're the only person who visits me, so I appreciate it when you can make it." Kaitlin's eyes glistened, and she turned her head away. David shook his head, willing his own tears to stay away.

It so easily could've been him on the other side of the table, had it not been for Robert taking him under his wing. He'd been too stoned to notice what Kaitlin was up to, other than making sure she was having a good time. He thought they'd both been having a good time, when in fact, it had been the worst time of their lives.

Sleeping in dirt near the Kurilpa Bridge, or passing out in an alleyway further in the city. Meeting food vans for breakfast and show- ering every third day at the drop-in centre in Fortitude Valley. Discarding their used syringes in the disposal containers in the public toilets. If only he'd made better choices. If only he'd been a better brother, then perhaps she wouldn't be sitting on the other side of the scratched metal table in prison greens.

"So, tell me what's new."

Sighing, David tried to cast aside his melancholy. It was difficult sharing about his life, because everything was tainted by guilt. Was it fair to share with Kaitlin about how much he loved his job, and how he got to experience the thrill of being outdoors every day? It was only by the grace of God he was able to enjoy such things. He didn't want Kaitlin returning to her cell with a cloud of depression hanging over her.

"Not much, really. Although, I met a guy the other day who does prison ministry." David shifted on his chair. To his knowledge, Kaitlin hadn't made a faith commitment. She had been somewhat receptive the times he'd spoken about God, but she still questioned his exis- tence. *Why had God allowed their mother to have children if she didn't care for them? And if God was so good, why did bad things happen to good people?*

Kaitlin arched her recently plucked brow. "I've seen those people around. They seem nice enough. Some of the girls have chats with them. I haven't been to the chapel though, or any of the Bible meetings they run."

That figures. He wanted to encourage her to give it a chance, but pressing the issue would most likely drive her further away. He would continue to pray, continue to visit and continue living his life so she might see Jesus.

"So, yeah … " David cleared his throat and smoothed over the top of his jeans. "He suggested opening up the business to ex-cons. Giving them something to do, building their self-esteem. That sort of thing."

"And are you gonna do it? It would mean more money for you, wouldn't it?"

"It's not about the money." David chuckled. Sure, he had bills and a mortgage to pay, but it had never been about making a quick buck.

"Don't tell me you actually love the work?" A coy grin broke on Kaitlin's face before she leaned forward, lowering her voice to a whisper. "I don't think anyone working here actually loves what they do."

David's shoulders convulsed, and he covered his mouth to contain his laughter.

"You are a rare breed, David. Oh!" Kaitlin squirmed on her chair and pulled something from the pocket in her track pants. A nearby guard frowned and stepped towards them, stopping only when Kaitlin pushed a piece of paper across the table.

"Check this out."

David's brow arched as he unfolded the paper and smoothed his fingers over the creases. His eyes travelled across the pencil lines. Dark and light. Thick and thin. "This is amazing."

"It is, hey."

The likeness was extraordinary. He ran his thumb across the structured cheek. Clear, soulful eyes stared back at him from the ivory paper.

"Who did this?"

"Gen. The girl who did my hair." She flicked her blonde locks over her shoulder.

"She's certainly got a gift. This is incredible." David perused the portrait again.

"Yeah, she's got other drawings – landscapes, structures around Brisbane, other portraits. Pretty cool, huh?"

"I'll say." The artist had captured the essence of her emotions, and the depth in Kaitlin's eyes tugged at his heart. The similarity between the portrait and his sister was startling. Swallowing the burn in his throat, he slid the picture across the table. Kaitlin placed her hand over his and squeezed.

"I want you to have it. As a reminder of your crazy sister."

"You're not crazy, Katy." David frowned at her self-deprecating talk. She shrugged in reply.

"Your opinion. Anyway, you can have it. And I think you should take that guy up on his offer. I reckon people will love it."

After saying their goodbyes, David watched the procession of green snake across the room as the officers led the prisoners away. David sniffed and drew a handkerchief from his pocket. It was never easy seeing his sister leave, knowing he had the freedom to get on with his life while she was still behind bars.

Pushing the chair back, David fell in behind the other visitors as they returned to the main entrance. He gathered his few belongings and stepped outside, squinting against the glare reflecting off the concrete. Closing his eyes, he lifted his face heavenward, basking in the warmth of the sun as he gave thanks for his freedom.

10

"We're heading out to the women's prison tomorrow." Tom and his wife Tricia sat across from David at Bean There, a coffee shop within walking distance of Elevation Adventures. David had prayed incessantly since Tom first introduced the idea over two weeks prior. He shared the idea with his colleagues, who expressed the same concerns David originally had. *What would it mean for the business? Would the prisoners pose a safety risk?* There were so many unknowns to work through, but his colleagues had agreed it was a great opportunity to branch out into community-based work.

David sipped his espresso, eyeing the older couple seated across from him. Tricia wore red-framed glasses and her chestnut hair was cut into a stylish bob. She was dwarfed by Tom's heavyset frame.

"We'll be given a list of women who are finishing their sentence. At chapel, we normally hand out cards with our details on them. I'll have a chat about what your role will be, and we'll go from there."

"That sounds good." David glanced down at Tom's business card. Nerves roiled in his stomach at the thought of meeting the prisoners. He'd walked alongside youths that were at-risk of offending. But the thought of being alongside prisoners, aside from his sister, sent his thoughts into chaos. He could be inviting arsonists, thieves, drug-dealers – even murderers – into his midst. He hadn't been far off prison himself, but *convicted criminals?* His mouth dried at the thought. Would they be putting other people at jeopardy? Would they put his business at risk?

Oh, Lord. Please give me the courage to accept this challenge you've placed before me. Help me to see it as an opportunity to reach people for you and to extend the same grace to them that was offered to me.

"You'll be safe when you go in." Tom's green eyes asserted kindness over the top of his coffee mug.

"Yes, yes, I know that." David nodded, running his fingers over Tom's card. "My ... my sister Katy is currently in prison. I visit her when I can, so I know a bit about how things work."

"Oh, I'm sorry to hear that." Surprise flickered across Tom's face, before empathy furrowed his brow.

"That must be hard on you." Tricia leaned forward, placing her hand over David's forearm.

"Yeah, it is tough." He exhaled and tugged on his sleeves, a conscious habit to hide the track marks permanently etched on his arms. Was now a good time to tell Tom and Tricia about his past? He hardly knew them and yet he probably owed it to him to be forthcoming with the truth.

"We'll definitely be praying for her." The warmth emulating from Tricia's smile triggered something inside.

"Thanks." He would share his story. Just not today.

"You're back!" Genevieve squealed and jumped to her feet, grabbing Karina's arms. The guard nodded abruptly before closing the cell door.

"What happened? Are you alright?" She stepped back, eyeing her friend.

Karina's hands enveloped Genevieve's. "I'm fine. I just copped a knock to the head and hit the deck."

"But how? What happened?" Genevieve perched on the edge of Karina's bed while Karina pulled the plastic chair over. Rumours were rife amongst the prisoners. Stories varied from someone sneaking a shiv into the room where the women worked on the headsets, to someone hassling a new inmate, and even women fighting over their exes.

Karina fluffed up her short hair. "Molly bad-mouthed the wrong person. And then both their sidekicks joined in. I was mindin' my own business, sortin' through the headsets, but just happened to be sittin' at the end of the table when the melee broke out, and I copped a knock to the head." Karina pointed to her temple. "Down I went. And of course, they panicked and sent me to hospital."

"Well, I'm so glad you're back. And by the looks of everything, you're okay." She wouldn't tell Karina how alone and afraid she'd felt without her there. It was silly how those feelings came flooding back after so long. Memories of her first night in the cell with Karina replayed, as she'd lain awake in the dark of night.

"You're a pretty thing, aren't ya." Karina sized her up when Genevieve was first shown to her cell. Timid and scared beyond belief, Karina's comment sent a chill through her bones. She needn't have worried, because Karina soon broke down her walls of mistrust and fear, showing Genevieve she was in fact, a gentle soul.

"Surprisingly, I have a brain!" Karina slapped her knees and threw her head back, her raw laughter filling the cell.

"I'm so glad to hear that!" Genevieve collapsed back onto the bed, joining in the laughter. It was good to have her friend back.

❦

Lunch consisted of another round of dry sandwiches, a withered salad and a carton of milk. Genevieve twirled the browning lettuce around the plastic utensil while Karina downed the last of her milk from the carton.

"Come join me in the chapel?" Karina wiped her mouth and moved over to the small basin next to the toilet. It wasn't the first time she'd asked. Karina often attended the chapel services, but Genevieve had never given them much thought. She was usually working in the salon, or doing some other activity.

Her idea of anything related to chapel invoked images of the compulsory services she attended at her exclusive religious high school, which were by far the most boring and conservative rituals she'd endured. Anything God-related didn't make sense. How could people believe in something, or someone, they couldn't see? How could one person supposedly make everything? And for someone to apparently die for the whole world – that just defied logic.

"Come on. We'll go together." Karina splashed water over her face and quickly patted it dry before draping the towel over the rail next to the basin.

"I don't …"

Karina looped her hand through Genevieve's arm, tugging her towards the door. "C'mon. It's not a confessional. There's no fire and brimstone. Tom and Tricia are lovely, if not the nicest, people you'll ever meet."

Genevieve stiffened and pulled back from Karina. What if they judged her? What if they scoffed at her, and ridiculed her for the poor choices she'd made? She deserved judgment, she knew that. She'd received it from her parents and the friends who'd abandoned her. But she'd found her safe place within the walls of the prison, and the friends she'd made all shared the same heartbreak and fear. She couldn't bear to face the derision of complete strangers.

"Gen." Karina turned around and placed her hands on Genevieve's shoulders. "You'll be fine. I'll be with you. Tom and Tricia are proof that there are carin' people out in the world. There's absolutely no expectation in there." Her eyes held compassion causing Genevieve to blink and look away. "If you're uncomfortable, we just get up and leave, okay?"

Genevieve nodded, already picturing them leaving midway through whatever Bible-bashing would be going on.

🐾 12 🐾

The chapel was a medium-sized room near the main entrance to the prison. Two fake potted palms stood in one corner. A small stained-glass window, depicting a cross, a dove and the sun's rays, filtered distorted light across a table at the front of the room. A simple wooden cross and black leather-bound Bible rested on the table.

Laughter and conversation floated across the peaceful room as Genevieve solemnly followed behind Karina. Her eyes darted around, noticing a few familiar faces.

"Ladies, we'll begin in five." Genevieve arched her neck to see where the deep male voice had come from. A tall, solid gentleman who looked to be around fifty stood in front of the table at the front of the room. His pale blue, short-sleeved button-up shirt highlighted his tanned skin. A woman of similar age sat in the front row of chairs. Her floral blouse was teamed with black jeans, and the tasseled earrings in her ears shook as she nodded her head.

Karina greeted a few of the women before walking to a row near the front. Genevieve held back, her heart hammered in her chest as she glanced around.

"Can we sit near the back?" She whispered to Karina. Overwhelming fear gripped her. She felt vulnerable and exposed.

"Sure, sure." Genevieve turned and led the way, sitting in the aisle seat in the second row from the back. It was only a short walk to the door if she needed to escape.

"Good morning!" The man who'd spoken earlier moved to the centre of the room. A warm smile stretched across his face as he made eye contact with each woman. Genevieve drew in a deep breath and smoothed her hands over her tracksuit pants. She crossed her ankles and tucked her feet underneath her chair.

"Let's open in prayer." He smiled again before closing his eyes.

"Dear Heavenly Father. I pray you will be with each of the women here today. Help them know you have a purpose for each of their lives. Help them to know how much they are loved by you ..."

Genevieve kept her eyes open as the man's voice, like warm molasses, settled over the room. Other women had their eyes closed. *What's the deal?*

The priests at her school used to pray, but it was nothing like the words coming from this man's mouth. Gentle and affirming. Aside from her high school years, she'd never spoken about God, or Jesus – unless one counted the numerous times she'd used His name as a curse word. How easy it just rolled off her tongue. But come to think of it, she'd never heard Karina use either name in a bad way.

She snuck a sideways glance at her cell mate who sat with her hands clasped together on her lap, a soft smile touching her lips, her eyes closed. Genevieve frowned and refocused her attention to the front of the room.

"It's so good to see you all again," the man announced. "And it's wonderful to have some newcomers joining us." His eyes roamed the room, a broad smile on his face. Genevieve quickly averted her gaze when his kind eyes landed on her.

"For those who don't know me, my name's Tom Matterson. My wife Tricia and I run the services here every week. Some weeks we'll sing. Other weeks we might spend less time singing and more time praying. Other weeks we'll just talk. We are completely led by what you need, and where we feel God leading us. We also help facilitate a Bible study for those who are interested."

"You should come," Karina whispered. Genevieve shrugged noncommittally. Did she want to go to a group and talk about fairy-tales and myths? Her sentence would be over soon, and she didn't want to start anything new. She just wanted to focus on getting out.

Words suddenly appeared on the white wall behind Tom, and music played from a speaker at the front of the room. Tricia stood up in the front row. Around the room, other women rose to their feet, while some remained seated.

Karina stood and began singing. Genevieve shifted to the edge of her chair, her hands gripping the seat in front of her. Should she stand? Should she remain seated? She glanced around as some women closed their eyes and raised their hands. What was she to do?

Karina gave her hand a squeeze. "It's okay," she whispered. "Just do what's comfortable for you." But she didn't know what was comfortable. The whole thing felt weird. It was peaceful, yet strange. It was nothing like she'd seen before. Chapel services during her teenage years had been dry and boring, and devoid of any emotion. But this was different. The music soaked through the pores of her hardened heart, evoking a calmness and peace she had never felt.

"I've invited a guest along today," Tom announced as the music finished and the women sat down. Low murmurs and wolf-whistles filled the air. Genevieve craned her neck to see past the heads blocking her view.

Tom's booming laugh bounced off the walls. "Now, now. Please don't embarrass the poor guy." Genevieve shifted on her seat. Her heart picked up pace as a figure moved forward to stand beside Tom.

Thick brown hair sat just above the collar of his shirt. She was too far away to see the colour of his eyes. Broad shoulders filled out the light-grey long-sleeved shirt hanging loosely over his blue jeans. Genevieve frowned. *That's so odd.* It was summer, and yet he was wearing long sleeves.

Laughing, Tom held up his hands. "Okay, okay. Everyone, I'd like you to meet David Molineaux." A few more wolf-whistles sounded, and a chorus of, "Hi David" echoed around the room.

"Hi everyone." David cleared his throat and clasped his hands in front of him, clearly looking uncomfortable with the attention. Genevieve slouched back against the chair and folded her arms.

"Tom asked me to come and have a chat about what I do." He cleared his throat again and shifted on his feet. "So, I, er ..." He ran a hand through his hair and glanced at Tom who gave an encouraging nod.

"I run a company called Elevation Adventures." David went on to speak about what the company did. Genevieve tuned out once David spoke of Brisbane.

Her thoughts carried her to another time – of picnics by the river. Catching the ferry with the wind flying through her hair. Lazy afternoons sprawled out on a picnic blanket at South Bank, lying on the white sand of the beach in the middle of the city. Then images of Ed flashed through her mind. The house they'd shared, the intimacy they once had. The baby she'd chosen to destroy.

A sharp pain shot through her chest, leaving her gasping. Genevieve pushed to her feet, and through a blur of tears, stumbled past the last row of chairs and pushed through the doors of the chapel.

Large sobs racked her body as she staggered around. Gulping for air, she leaned over, resting her hands on her knees. Memories of her past mistakes slammed into her. Ed. The drinking. The drugs. The baby she'd destroyed. The policeman's bloodied face after she'd punched him out of anger, because she'd been too wasted to know any better.

Slumping down against the wall, tears streamed down her face. The cold concrete seeped through her thin tracksuit. Her body shook in anguish as she drew her knees to her chest. She thought she'd dealt with her failures since being incarcerated. She thought she'd moved on from her past. So why now, of all times, was it suffocating the life out of her?

❦ 13 ❦

"**G**en?" The chapel door opened, and Tricia followed behind Karina as they walked over, sitting on either side of Genevieve as she huddled in the corner of the building.

"What's wrong, love?" Karina placed her arm around Genevieve's trembling shoulders.

"Nothing." She sniffed, wiping her nose on the sleeve of her jumper.

"I'm Tricia." Placing her hand on Genevieve's arm, the other woman offered a warm smile. "It can all seem a bit overwhelming when you come for the first time." She tilted her head towards the chapel before handing Genevieve a handful of tissues. Genevieve nodded her thanks as she continued to whimper.

It wasn't so much the chapel service that overwhelmed her. It was the relentless reminders of her past. She was an intelligent woman. How had she made such stupid choices?

"Karina tells me you're a very good artist. What do you draw?" Tricia's smiling face came into view. Her eyes crinkled behind the glasses perched on her nose.

Genevieve narrowed her eyes at Karina as her face flushed. "Different things. Landscapes. Sometimes people." A sob escaped at the

48

thought of her drawings. The pictures of the child she'd never meet, because she'd been too selfish to care.

"I paint," Tricia said. "I'm not that great at it, but I enjoy it. We live near Moreton Bay, so I often take my easel and some water paints down by the sea and paint whatever takes my fancy. Sometimes I have a plan, sometimes I don't."

Genevieve sniffed, wiping her eyes on a tissue. "I don't normally have a plan. I just draw. Mostly places I used to frequent before ..." She waved her hand around, unable to utter the words.

"It's a good way to get your mind off things." Tricia smiled kindly. "Painting helps me relax. Has anyone else seen your drawings?"

Pressing her lips together, Genevieve shook her head. "Mainly Karina. I've done a few portraits for some of the other women here, but no one else."

"What about family, or friends?"

Genevieve blew her nose and sighed. "I used to spend hours drawing as a kid. My mother would always say I was wasting my time, that my art would never get me anywhere." She gave an abrupt laugh. "I bet she didn't think I'd end up in here when I was studying law. I haven't seen her since I was sentenced."

"I'm sorry to hear that. Try not to blame yourself, though." Tricia's genuine compassion seeped through Genevieve's hardened façade, invoking another wave of tears. "I know prison might seem like the last place to find people who care about you, but we're here. I know it's not the same as having your parents support. We all desire that connection. Deep down, we all have a need to feel accepted and loved. And when those closest to us fail to offer that, it hurts way more than we expect."

"My parents only cared about their reputation, and making sure I was following what they wanted. One step wrong and they completely disowned me." Genevieve drew a deep breath and shuddered, recalling the look of contempt upon her mother's face when she visited the house she shared with Ed.

It had been wonderful being away from the rigidity of the house on Hamilton Hill, with its security cameras and overbearing iron gates that separated the Trehearn's from the rest of the world. Genevieve overlooked the dirty dishes and grimy floors when she became busy with exams, or when she was too hungover to care. And when the drugs became a daily ritual, she just swept things off the coffee table to participate in the momentary highs.

It was the only time she'd felt free – if only for a fleeting moment to escape the strict and oppressive upbringing her parents imposed on her. Somehow, she managed to function – attending university and passing her exams – but her relationship with Ed became volatile, and the strangers invading the home they shared began to scare her.

She could've walked away – she *should* have – but she hadn't known where to go. She'd convinced herself she was in love with Ed, only realizing now she was in love with the idea of being loved. She couldn't blame Ed for her downfall. She was naïve, and desperate enough to be lured by his charm as a means to escape the gilded cage she was trapped in.

"You're not alone, Genevieve." Tricia's soothing voice drew her away from the sombre path her thoughts were taking.

"I feel so alone," Genevieve whispered, biting at the quick of her thumbnail. "Sorry, Karina." She offered an apologetic smile to her only true friend.

"No need to apologize, Gen. I get it. I felt terribly alone at times. Gosh, the things I've done in my life would be enough to scare anyone away." Karina pulled a leaf off a nearby shrub and twirled it in her fingers. "But I've learned that I'm never alone, because God is with me. He's the only reason I'm still here."

Genevieve eyed her friend in disbelief.

"Not many people know this. Tom and Tricia do. As do the guards who were involved." Karina crossed her legs and pressed her back against the concrete wall. "When I first came here all those years ago, I was on suicide watch for two weeks. I was an absolute mess."

Genevieve's mouth dropped open. "I didn't know that." She always thought Karina had it together. She wasn't rough like some of the other women. And she carried an air of positivity wherever she went.

Karina smoothed her hands over the concrete and shrugged. "It's not something I share with everyone. Can you imagine? 'Hey, guess what? I tried to slash my wrists and slice my throat! And because that didn't work, I tried to use a bed sheet to end my life.' I don't think that would go down too well."

Too shocked to move or say anything, Genevieve eyed her friend.

"But Tom and Tricia sat outside my cell each day and prayed continuously. They didn't try to shove the Bible down my throat. They just came and prayed. Sometimes out loud. Sometimes just between the two of them." Karina surreptitiously wiped a tear from the corner of her eye. "I didn't understand why they'd bother comin' to see the likes of me. I mean, no one in my family bothered, so why would they?"

Just like my family. Why would anyone else care, when they can't even manage a visit in almost three years?

"But then they introduced me to Jesus, and showed me His love – by visitin' and prayin', acceptin' me and not judgin'. I figured this Jesus guy must be okay, and decided to find out for myself." A wistful smile danced on Karina's serene face.

Swallowing the lump in her throat, Genevieve turned her head away. Her eyes burned, and she felt the warmth of Tricia's hand close around her arm. Soft, comforting words floated around as both Tricia and Karina prayed. Was there really hope for her?

⌘

DAVID CONTINUED TO GLANCE TOWARDS THE DOOR, WONDERING what the commotion was about. Tricia had followed the two women outside, and he was curious to know what had transpired. It was awkward enough addressing a roomful of women, acknowledging their imprisonment. And then for two women to leave – perhaps he wasn't cut out for this after all.

"You don't need to tiptoe around it," Tom leaned over and whispered, sensing David's unease. "They all know they'll be released soon. We've spoken with them about the process, and the program we offer outside. You're just letting them know about something else for them to add purpose to their lives."

Distracted by the look of distress on the brunette's face as she left the room, David drew a deep breath and toyed with the keys in his pocket.

"Dave?" Tom glanced his way before turning to address the remaining women. "On your release, you'll be given our contact details. We'll be working alongside Dave here to take you on some outdoor adventures. Who's excited?"

A raucous cheer went up, interspersed with a few expletives. Thighs were slapped. High-fives were given. David's eyebrows rose and his face warmed at the chaotic scene. Tom shrugged and grinned. "God's grace," he mouthed.

David nodded, scanning the room. He certainly knew about that. If God could show him grace, by sparing his life and sparing him from the black mark of a prison sentence, then surely he could extend the same grace towards these women. *It's not about me. These women need God as much as I do.*

Straightening his shoulders, he drew a breath, ready to step into whatever adventure God had in store for him.

❧ 15 ❧

Sleep evaded her. No matter how many times she closed her eyes, repositioned, counted sheep, or placed the covers over her head, sleep was elusive.

With a sigh, Genevieve crossed her hands behind her head and stared at the ceiling. A dull glow from the lamps outside the cell cast shadows along the wall.

Who is this Jesus guy? How can he help me?

After the chapel service finished, Tricia shared more about Jesus, and how much he loved her. Genevieve couldn't understand how someone could love her after everything she'd done. And yet, Tricia's words triggered something deep within.

She cringed with a distant memory of some street preachers in the Queen Street Mall. It was night. They'd popped some pills before heading into the city. She vaguely recalled someone handing out brochures near one of the street corners. Ed snatched one out of the man's hand, and then tossed it into the air as they walked past. Ed called out some expletives over his shoulder, and said something about God being a fairytale that only crazies believed in. They'd both laughed and stumbled their way through the nighttime crowd, people parting to make way for the drug-addled pair.

Tears wet her cheeks. Gosh, she'd been so stupid. Shame washed over her as she thought of the poor street preacher and how they'd ridiculed him.

But, if God is good, why did He allow bad things to happen? Why did He allow my parents to disregard me? Does He really care like Tricia and Karina say? And what was with the singing?

The songs were like nothing she'd heard before. They were certainly like nothing on the radio. They weren't aggressive, and they didn't proclaim subtle innuendos. Rather, the words spoke of peace, love and forgiveness. Something about being washed clean and having sins removed as far as the east is from the west. What did that mean? And what did it mean to be truly forgiven?

Her shoulders shook as tears streamed down her face with the memory of Tricia's gentle voice. She had never known such compassion from a stranger. And the younger guy ... he seemed nice too. Her brow twitched as she recalled his long sleeves.

With her mind adrift in a fog of chaotic thoughts, Genevieve rolled onto her side, pressing her back against the concrete wall, and willed sleep to come.

❧ 16 ❧

David spent the remainder of the week in planning mode. Rain teemed down outside, tapping a staccato on the tin roof of the patio. The day's bookings were cancelled due to the inclement weather. That was a downside of owning an outdoor adventure business. The positive was that he was able to catch up on paperwork at home and plan for their upcoming outings.

Running a hand through his hair, David pushed back from the laptop at the kitchen table as his thoughts returned to the women's prison. He'd really mucked that up. His nerves were on full display, and he hadn't made Elevation Adventures sound anywhere near as exciting as it was. No doubt all the women would have laughed at him as he bumbled his way through the presentation. Thankfully, he hadn't seen Katy in there. He didn't particularly want the other women to know they were related, in case she suffered the repercussions of his incompetence.

Tom had suggested an outing with the women in four weeks' time. They would have a couple of weeks to adjust to life outside bars, before incorporating a day's adventure alongside their assimilation back into society.

David blew out a breath and leaned back in the chair, folding his hands behind his head. A low purr sounded, and his wandering cat sidled up against his legs.

"BC! What have you been up to?" David bent down and scooped up the cat, plucking some grass out of her black hair. The cat narrowed her eyes, before turning around and settling onto David's lap.

"Do you think I can do this, BC? I'm a bit nervous about hosting a group of ex-prisoners. I'm not too sure if I'm going to be able to live up to Tom's expectations." The cat flicked her ears and tossed her head, as though rebuffing David's comment. "Yeah. Thanks for your support."

David spent a few more moments jotting things down in his diary before BC jumped to the ground and padded away. Brushing the stray black hairs from his shorts, David closed the laptop. He grabbed his keys and a bottle of water before flicking off the house lights, closing the front door and jogging to his ute in the driveway.

Leaning over the dashboard, David wiped condensation off the inside of the windscreen with an old towel. The wipers squeaked on the outside, leaving a smear of grime as they traversed the glass. Gripping the steering wheel, David peered through the hazy windscreen as he cautiously navigated the wet roads towards the indoor climbing centre.

Fifteen minutes later, he whipped into an empty parking space outside a large warehouse. Rain needled his skin and soaked his shirt as he dashed across the bitumen.

"Dave." Joshua Rixon, one of his closest friends, walked over as he entered the building.

"Hey, Josh." The pair clasped hands and patted each other on the shoulder.

"Crazy weather out there today."

David nodded as he sat down, slipping off his wet sneakers before pulling on a pair of rock climbing shoes. "Yeah, I know. We had to cancel a number of bookings. Not sure about tomorrow yet."

Stepping into some harnesses, the men secured the straps around their waist and attached small pouches of chalk powder to their belts.

Given the persistent rain outside, the indoor rock climbing centre wasn't as busy as David anticipated. With three levels of difficulty to choose from, the pair set up in front of the wall suited to more experienced climbers.

"You wanna go up first?" David asked, eyeing the wall in front of them.

"Yeah, sure." They connected the ropes to their carabiners, and Josh began scaling the wall while David stood below, belaying the ropes. It wasn't the same as climbing the Kangaroo Point Cliffs, but at least it was exercise and he wasn't cooped up inside his house.

As he allowed the rope to run through his hands, his thoughts turned to Tom and Tricia.

This is so crazy, Lord. Who am I even to consider taking prisoners out? I know you want me to do it, but why?

"You good down there?" Josh called as he leaned out from the wall.

David glanced up and loosened the rope behind his back. "Yeah, sorry. Just got distracted."

"No worries." Josh chuckled and continued climbing. After reaching the top, he abseiled down and David took his turn to scale the wall.

An hour passed with both men alternating climbs. It was a good workout, and David's muscles ached by the time they finished. Dripping in sweat, the men stepped out of their harnesses and returned the equipment to the rental counter.

"So I've been asked to lead a women's prison group with the company." David leaned down and slipped off his shoes. Stretching out his feet, he enjoyed the brief freedom and rush of air over his toes before stepping into his running shoes.

"And?" Josh arched an eyebrow as he removed his gloves and tossed them onto the table.

"I don't know. I'm a bit worried, to be honest. I'm not sure I'm up to the task. I don't even know why I was asked." David leaned forward, clasping his hands in front of him.

Josh wiped over his face with a towel. "Because you're the right person. Take a chance on them, Dave. You don't need to see the bigger picture, or know all the whys. You just need to take the next step."

Sighing, David glanced across at his friend. "You're right." Why did he continue to doubt? Why did he continue to believe he wasn't good enough?

"Don't let fear hold you back."

And that's just what it was. Fear. Fear he wasn't good enough. Fear people would think he was a hypocrite. Fear people would judge him. Fear he'd be attacked, or the business would suffer. He called himself a Christian, but where was his faith? And was it really faith if he didn't take action?

"You know, I can't think of anyone better to be leading those groups." Josh folded his hands behind his head revealing sweat marks on his shirt. The noise level in the centre increased as a few other groups arrived to make the most of the unfavourable weather.

Reaching across the table, David grabbed a sugar packet and twirled it between his fingers.

"God doesn't call the qualified ..."

"Yeah, yeah." David shook his head, waving Josh's comment away. "He qualifies the called. I've heard it before."

"And?" Josh folded his arms and quirked an eyebrow, a coy grin playing on his lips. David tossed the sugar packet aside and leaned his elbows on the table. Running his hands through his damp hair, he sighed.

"The truth is, I'm scared. Pure and simple." Doubts constantly plagued him. The same questions taunted him repeatedly. *What if I'm not good enough? What if I mess up? Who am I to guide others with such a tainted past?* He tugged at the sleeves on his top, the ink and scars a constant reminder of his messed up life.

"Mate, every step of faith is scary. That's why it's called faith. It's stepping out into the unknown, trusting God for the next step."

He *knew* that. But was he willing to act on it? David looked around at the various artificial rock walls in the centre, his eyes were drawn to the climbing holds spaced sporadically up the walls. Climbers only ever took one step at a time, and often they couldn't see their final destination.

Chuckling, he lifted a bottle of water to his lips. Faith was no different. God certainly had a way of grabbing his attention.

❧ 17 ❧

Butterflies roiled in Genevieve's stomach, keeping her awake. She tossed and turned on the mattress.

"You alright up there?" Karina's groggy voice broke through the dark.

"Yes, sorry. Just can't sleep."

"You nervous about tomorrow?" The mattress groaned as Karina moved on her bed.

"I guess." Genevieve exhaled. Lying on her back, she watched shadows dance across the ceiling. The day she'd been dreaming of since she'd first arrived at the Women's Correctional Centre was almost upon her. Oh, how she'd dreamed of this moment. But now, with freedom looming, she was nervous and couldn't fight the anxiety whirling within. What would she do? What would her parents say? Would they even want to see her? And what about money? How would she afford to live?

The social worker had guided her through the release process. She would be given a bank card which would give her access to her earnings as a hairdresser while in prison. That would tide her over for some time before welfare kicked in, but beyond that – she had no clue. She didn't want to remain on welfare. But, who would employ an ex-con?

"God's got it sorted, Gen. Just remember that."

God. If she couldn't trust those she could see, how was it possible to trust someone she couldn't see? Perhaps it was worth a shot. She had nothing to lose – she'd lost everything the moment she stepped foot inside the prison.

Her spirit had been broken, her self-esteem shattered. And all she wanted was to feel whole. To feel worth. To stop feeling helpless and utterly hopeless.

She'd attended chapel twice more with Karina, observing everything that went on. The words of the songs and the prayers offered by Tom and Tricia stirred something within her. They talked about forgiveness and becoming a new creation.

She'd seen changes in some of the women. They were softer and exuded an inner peace, despite their circumstances. And she wanted that for herself. She was tired of feeling the relentless churning of angst. She was tired of feeling broken and empty.

"Karina," she whispered into the darkness of the cell.

"Yes, love?"

"Sorry I've kept you awake."

"That's okay. What's bothering you?"

Genevieve smiled at Karina's ever-gentle tone, and curled onto her side, resting her hands underneath her cheek.

"Do you think God loves me?"

Karina's feet hit the floor with a thud, and her face soon appeared at the side of Genevieve's bunk.

"I don't think He loves you. I *know* He does." Her voice was fierce, yet gentle.

"How can you be so sure?"

"Because I believe what the Bible tells me. And I know it here," she tapped her head. "And here." She rested a hand over her heart. "I've changed, Gen. I'm not the same woman I was all those years ago. And it's all because of God."

Genevieve rolled onto her back. A single tear escaped and trickled down the side of her cheek. "But how could he love *me*? I ..." A sob escaped before she clasped a hand over her mouth. "I killed my baby."

"Oh, love." Karina's large hand smoothed over Genevieve's forehead, brushing strands of hair back from her face. Soothing her. Calming her. Being the motherly figure she'd never known. Pressing her lips together, Genevieve tried to contain the sobs of anguish over the secret she'd harboured for so long.

"You're the first person I've told, besides Ed."

"Thank you for trustin' me," Karina continued smoothing her hair. "That can't have been easy for you."

Genevieve shook her head, closing her eyes to fight off the horrors of that day. The fear. The shame. The emptiness of the aftermath.

Because of the drugs, Ed had already been pulling away from her, distancing himself. And she was desperate to do everything in her power to keep him. She would have done anything for someone to love her, and so she'd sacrificed a child to keep what she thought was the love of her life. What a fool she'd been.

In the weeks and months afterwards, she grieved in silence. For years she harboured her horrific secret. Emptiness consumed her, and she numbed her pain with a drug-induced altered reality. People who protested for a woman's right to choose had no idea about the emotional turmoil she'd endured. She was a murderer, pure and simple.

"God loves you, regardless of what you've done. He knows your past, your secrets, your hurts. And yet, He still loves you. His love for you is unconditional and like nothing any human can offer you. He made you and has wonderful plans for your life."

"I just want ..." Gen's voice was thick with emotion. "I just want to be free. I want to feel peace, instead of this constant worry and angst that I carry around with me."

Karina found Genevieve's hand in the dark, giving it a gentle, reassuring squeeze. "Can I pray for you?"

"Yes please," she whispered, gripping Karina's hands in her own.

Genevieve closed her eyes while Karina prayed. Tears flowed uninhibited as the words washed over her, infusing her with peace and stilling her anxious thoughts.

Wiping her tears on her pillow, Genevieve whispered her thanks. Karina pulled her into an embrace and placed a kiss on her forehead.

"You're welcome. I hope you can get a good sleep tonight. Tomorrow's the start of a new life for you."

Tonight. Tonight's the start of a new life for me.

"Thanks. Sleep well too. I'm sorry for disturbing you." Genevieve squeezed Karina's hand before she climbed down and settled back into her own bed.

"Don't apologise. I'm glad you were able to talk to me."

Soft snores soon floated up from Karina's bed. Genevieve smiled and closed her eyes.

God, Jesus – what do I call you? I guess that's something I'll have to figure out. I've seen the changes in some of the women here, and even Karina told me she's changed. I want that for myself. I want to change. I want to be a better person. I want the hope that you offer – the hope that Tom and Tricia, and Karina have spoken about. Hope, not just for now, but also my future. I don't want to be afraid anymore.

I know I've messed up. Big time. But, maybe they're right in saying you offer forgiveness for all my bad stuff. I hope so. Because I am so sorry for what I've done. For the people I've hurt. For the lies I've told. For the life I've taken. Please forgive me.

It feels so wrong asking you to forgive me for what I've done, but I can't live with all the turmoil anymore. It's hard to believe that someone would die for me – because I am so not worth anyone dying for. But apparently you did, and I want to say thank you for that.

Genevieve pulled her sleeve over her fingers and wiped her eyes, before pulling the bedcovers up to her chin. Her body felt light, her eyelids heavy as she succumbed to the last few hours of sleep before she would be a free woman.

18

"I'm gonna miss you so much." With tears shimmering in her eyes, Karina pulled Genevieve into a tight embrace.

"I'm going to miss you too," Genevieve murmured against Karina's shoulder. "Thanks for everything. You've been a good room mate." Karina's body shook as a rumble of laughter filled the air.

Picking up her notebook and drawing utensils, along with her small pile of belongings, Genevieve took one last look around the concrete cell that had been her home for the past three years.

"I want to give you this." Karina sat her worn black leather-bound Bible on top of Genevieve's belongings.

"But, what about you?"

Karina waved her hand. "I'll get another one from Tom or Tricia. It's more important that you have it now."

Genevieve blinked away the sting of tears. "Thank you. I don't know what else to say."

"Come on Trehearn." The guard at the door cleared his throat.

"See you Karina. Thanks for everything."

"Write to me. We can be pen-pals!"

"Will do." Genevieve turned and smiled at her friend, standing all alone in the cell. "And I'll come and visit."

"Make sure you do." Karina grinned before vigorously wiping an eye. "Go on. Before you see me collapse in a sobbing heap."

Genevieve followed the guard, before turning one last time to wave to her closest friend. Committing Karina's weathered, yet kind, face to memory, she followed the guard along the corridor.

She wanted to commit everything to memory – the way the fourth light from her cell flickered; the peeling paint on the off-white walls; the etching on the doors in the common room; the mix of smells in the herb and vegetable garden. She wanted to remember it all, simply to remind herself of who she once was.

She wasn't the same angry and humiliated woman who'd stepped into the prison three years ago, having her dignity and physical possessions stripped away.

The guard opened the door and led her to a small room where she was given a black plastic bag, containing her purse, the clothes and shoes she'd worn into prison, and her mobile phone. She quickly changed out of her green tracksuit, thankful to see the last of it, and vowing to never wear that shade of green again. Slipping her feet into the sandals, she wriggled her toes, enjoying the freedom of movement after being cramped into the prison-issue sneakers for so long.

Another prison officer handed her a piece of paper - her release certificate - and walked her outside to a metal gate.

"Good luck."

Genevieve hesitated before turning to the officer, a question on her lips. Devoid of emotion, he nodded. "You're free to go."

Sucking in a breath, Genevieve smoothed down the front of her wrinkled black pants and stepped out of the gate. Traffic noise from the motorway drifted across the almost-full parking lot. She took a few steps forward before glancing over her shoulder. The gate was already closed and the guard nowhere to be seen. For a brief moment, she wanted to run back and demand to be let back in.

The razor wired loomed large around the perimeter of the prison. It seemed surreal viewing it from her vantage point on the footpath outside.

I'm free! Laughter bubbled up and Genevieve threw her head back, soaking in the warmth of the sun upon her face. *I'm free! I'm free!* A car horn sounded, and she opened her eyes as a silver sedan pulled up nearby.

"Hi, Gen! You all ready?" Tricia opened the front passenger door and stepped out. Walking over, she pulled Genevieve into an embrace. "It's so good to see you. How are you feeling?"

"I'm ..." Genevieve shook her head, unable to contain the grin on her face. "I'm so happy. I'm excited. I'm scared. I'm nervous. I'm ... free!"

"You are! And it's so wonderful!" Tricia squeezed her arms and grinned. Her dark bob swaying as she laughed.

"Hey Gen!" Tom leaned over the passenger seat and waved.

"Ready?" Tricia opened the back door and Genevieve slid in. Tossing her bag on the seat beside her, she clasped her hands on her lap and gazed out the window, refusing to look behind her, as Tom drove off.

The surrounds were unfamiliar to Genevieve – she'd never ventured over this side of town before, having spent her childhood on the north side of the river. Rows of eucalyptus trees flashed by, giving way to a new estate of houses.

Soon they were on the motorway, heading towards the city. Tom caught her eye in the rearview mirror – his eyes crinkled at the corners as he smiled. He merged right and drove down a ramp leading into a tunnel. Genevieve straightened and clutched the seatbelt. "Where are we going?"

"This is a new tunnel that bypasses all the city traffic. It only opened recently." Tricia turned in her seat, offering Genevieve a reassuring smile. Lights flickered along the roof of the tunnel, reminding Genevieve of her final walk through the prison. She closed her eyes to block out the view, but the orange glow of the lights pierced through her eyelids filled her with trepidation.

❧ 19 ❧

"Here we are," Tricia announced a short while later as Tom pulled the car into the driveway of a humble low-set house.

Genevieve grabbed her plastic bag of belongings and opened the car door, tentatively stepping out.

Telephone wires looped between poles up and down the street. A light breeze blew, rustling the leaves in the well-established trees along the footpath of the older suburb with an eclectic mix of single and double storey homes.

"We're just a short walk from the water." Tricia pointed towards the end of the street. "Three blocks that way."

Genevieve nodded, toting her bag as she followed Tom and Tricia up the path.

"How long have you lived here?"

"About twenty years. It's wonderful being able to go for walks along the waterfront. And like I said, I take my paints down there too."

A tremor of excitement ran through Genevieve as she contemplated the endless possibilities awaiting her.

Once inside, Tom excused himself to make some phone calls. The house was comfortably decorated. Sheer curtains covered the front living room windows. A three-seater couch with two armchairs were set up around a coffee table with a bowl of decorative rattan balls as the centrepiece.

"Bedrooms and bathroom are down that way." Tricia gestured to her left before she opened a sliding glass door and stepped out onto a timber deck that ran along the length of the house. To the right was a large wooden table and matching bench seats. Two wicker couches with aqua blue cushions and a matching coffee table made a cosy nook to the left.

Three steps led down to the grass and across a gravel path to a smaller building clad in light blue weatherboard with a white tin roof. A potted fern sat by the front door. Tricia inserted a key in the door and pushed it open.

"Welcome." She ushered Genevieve inside and grinned. "I hope you like it."

Dropping her bag to the floor, Genevieve slowly turned around, taking in the beach-themed décor. Tears welled in her eyes at Tricia and Tom's generosity.

The granny flat in their back yard had been empty for sometime. They usually offered it to missionaries on furlough, or visitors to their church. They'd only housed two ex-prisoners prior to Genevieve.

"Thank you," she whispered, her voice catching in her throat. "This is …. more than I could have ever hoped for."

Tricia gave her a quick tour of the granny-flat, comprising of a combined kitchen and lounge area, one bathroom and her bedroom.

"We'll share the laundry. And you can join us for dinner tonight. I'll take you shopping tomorrow. After that, we try and encourage the women to do things for themselves. That way, you can establish your own routine, and work out what's best for you. But, we're always a phone call, or a door knock away."

"Thank you." Smiling, Genevieve clutched her hands to her chest. This was real. The thought of being on her own both excited and terrified her.

After Tricia left, Genevieve wandered around the small flat, unable to wipe the smile off her face. There was even a chair and table on the front porch for her to sit on. A perfect place to draw.

Thank you, God. The prayer slipped out, catching her unaware. *Yes, it must have been God. Because I really don't deserve this. If this is what God and Jesus is all about – loving others unconditionally and hope for the future, then I want that.*

Genevieve unpacked her few belongings and tossed the plastic bag from prison into the bin before slipping off her sandals and preparing for a shower.

Tricia had stocked the bathroom with body wash, a loofah, moisturizer, and other delectable toiletries. Genevieve lingered under the spray of water, savouring the freedom and privacy of a normal shower as she washed away the physical remnants of her imprisonment.

Drying off, she changed into some shorts and a t-shirt Tricia had purchased for her. The styles weren't to Genevieve's usual taste, but she couldn't be fussy when they had been generously provided for her.

The afternoon sun shone down as she stepped out onto the porch with her notebook and pencils. Birdsong carried on the breeze. A mix of palm and eucalyptus trees stretched tall above the neighbouring fences. How good it was not to see the razor wire or the concrete compounds she was accustomed to.

The sun warmed her arms as she jotted down a list of food, clothing and other supplies she needed. Flipping to a new page, she wrote down another list of things to do. She would have to ask Tricia and Tom about public transport, and would need to find work that was easily accessible by bus or train.

And then there was the issue of her parents. A sinking feeling settled in the pit of her stomach. Would they want to see her? *Forget about them now. Just focus on today. Wasn't that what Karina had once said? Don't worry about tomorrow? Give it all to God? I'm trying not to worry. God, if you're there, please take my anxious thoughts away.*

AFTER ENJOYING HER FIRST HOME-COOKED MEAL IN A LONG TIME, Genevieve excused herself from Tom and Tricia's company and returned to her new home. The street was quiet, with only the occasional car passing by. It would take some getting used to the different sounds. No more banging on walls from other prisoners. No more wailing. No more alarms.

Crawling into the double bed, Genevieve nestled into the comfortable mattress and breathed in the fresh scent of laundry powder. The sheets were soft and didn't scratch her skin like the ones in prison. It was all so surreal. Perhaps it was just a dream. Perhaps she was going to wake up tomorrow and find herself back in the prison cell.

Karina's Bible caught her eye from the bedside table. Genevieve shimmied into a sitting position and pulled it onto her lap, not knowing what to do. She ran her fingers over the pages, enjoying the feel of the soft paper underneath her fingertips. Should she start at the beginning, or just open it up somewhere? She flicked open to a page, not knowing what the numbers meant. Moving her fingers along the words, she suddenly stopped.

In my distress I prayed to the Lord, and the Lord answered me and set me free.

Genevieve's heart pounded. *What?* She read the words again. *Who is this about? What's their story? What do they need to be set free from?* She devoured the previous paragraphs, before grabbing her notebook and pen and jotting down the numbers on the page, intending to ask Tricia about their meaning.

She reread the words. *In my distress, the Lord answered me. He set me free. Yes, He did! I am free!*

She kicked her feet excitedly underneath the covers before returning Karina's Bible to the table. Filled with hope, Genevieve flicked off the bedside lamp and nestled into the comfortable bed. With her heart full of gratitude, sleep came easily.

❧ 20 ❧

Her first two weeks of freedom flew by. Tricia had taken Genevieve to the nearby shopping mall to purchase clothing and other necessities. It was strange stepping foot inside a shopping centre again. She'd frequented them quite regularly in her previous life. Shopping and beauty salons were all a part of her weekly routine. Now, she couldn't care less about those things.

She'd purchased a new wardrobe – enough clothes so she could mix and match, some new toiletries and shoes. And she'd paid a visit to the hairdressers. Her split ends were tidied up and she had layers added, allowing her chestnut brown tresses to fall softly around her face.

Being in public had terrified her, as though everyone would know she was an ex-prisoner. But Tricia provided constant reassurance and encouragement, allaying any insecurities that arose.

Over lunch, Tricia spoke of her involvement with the prison ministry, and also the church they attended. Sipping her cappuccino, the first since her incarceration, Genevieve listened intently, the concept of church still so foreign to her.

"Our church is fundraising for a mission trip to Thailand." Tricia settled back in her seat and stirred the flat white in front of her. "We'll be sending some people over to work in the orphanages over there. I normally go, but I won't be this year. Instead, I'm helping organise a dinner and silent auction to raise money."

Genevieve sipped her coffee, relishing the creaminess of milk on her tongue as Tricia explained about the silent auction.

"I think you should enter some of your artwork for the auction." Tricia slid her glasses up her nose. "But only if you feel comfortable doing so."

Genevieve's face warmed at the idea and she tightened her grip on the cup as she pondered Tricia's suggestion. The thought of her private drawings on public display filled her with apprehension. Karina had suggested she sell her work, but nothing had eventuated because Genevieve hadn't pursued it. Drawing was her passion, and a means to pour out her emotions and escape her thoughts. But was her art something people would pay money for?

"Have a think about it, anyway. It will be a fun night, and a great way for you to meet new people," Tricia said. That was last week. And now, Saturday had arrived.

Genevieve looked in the full-length mirror against the back of her bedroom door. Her hair sat loose around her shoulders, the freshly-cut layers hanging softly around her face. She twisted from side-to-side, smiling at the cobalt-blue sleeveless dress that rested just above her knees. The skirt swished around her legs, and paired with strappy white sandals, looked summery. After being accustomed to a tracksuit for so long, it felt nice to be wearing a dress.

A light coating of foundation, mascara and lip gloss completed her appearance. Before jail, Genevieve would spend hours getting ready to go out. Now, with a renewed perspective, she didn't feel the inclination to do so. Tucking her white purse under one arm, she smoothed over her stomach, willing her nerves to settle.

❦

PENNINSULA COMMUNITY CHURCH OVERLOOKED THE PEACEFUL waters of the bay. Set back from the road, a parking lot extended across the front of the property. Garden beds full of colourful flowers bordered a concrete path leading to the front of the brick building.

Jazz music and the low hum of conversation filled the air as Genevieve followed Tom and Tricia into the church hall. Genevieve glanced around the room and froze. A trickle of sweat ran between her shoulder blades. She hadn't expected so many people. *They're going to know. It's obvious I have no clue what to do, and they're going to know I've spent the last three years in prison.*

Sensing her discomfort, Tricia stepped back and looped her hand through Genevieve's arm. "It's okay. You're safe, Gen. I'll introduce you to some people. You'll be okay."

Genevieve nodded, clutching her purse in front of her. How would Tricia introduce her? *Hi, everyone. This is Genevieve. She's just been released from prison. Yeah, like that will go down well.*

Tables decorated with votive candles and floral centrepieces were set up in rows across the middle of the room. Various items for sale or auction were displayed around the perimeter.

"Dianne, I want to introduce you to a friend of mine." Tricia tugged Genevieve forward. Smoothing over the skirt of her dress, she plastered a smile on her face as a woman of similar age to Tricia turned around. Her brown hair was styled into a chignon and her hazel eyes sparkled with her smile.

"This is Genevieve. Genevieve, Dianne."

"Nice to meet you, Genevieve. How do you two know each other?"

Genevieve opened and closed her mouth, darting a glance at Tricia. Shifting on her feet, she eyed the exit, wondering how long it would take her to get to the other side of the room.

"Through a mutual friend," Tricia replied. "Genevieve's an amazing artist. Some of her work is up for auction tonight."

"Oh that's wonderful!" Dianne smiled, tucking her tan leather purse under her arm. "Well, it's nice to meet you. I'll have to keep an eye out for your work."

"Thank you. You too," Genevieve replied, her eyes flicking across to the exit again. Tricia guided her away from the crowd to a vacant area near the displays of handmade jewellery.

"Did you just lie for me?" Genevieve whispered.

"No, because we did meet through a mutual friend – Karina. People don't need to know your story when you first meet. If and when it's

73

meant to be told, the time will come for that." Genevieve's shoulders sagged in relief. She should have trusted Tricia's discretion.

"Oh, look! There's David." Genevieve trailed behind as Tricia wound her way through a cluster of people, and to an opening in front of a display of an assortment of pottery bowls and vases and, she swallowed, three of her drawings. They looked so different in frames. As though they had been drawn by a professional artist. The paper was pure white and creaseless, unlike her worn notebook at home. A smile touched her lips as an unexpected feeling of pride welled within.

Standing in front of her artwork was a man who looked vaguely familiar. His brown hair sat just above the collar of his grey long-sleeve shirt. Broad shoulders filled the soft material, and his jeans fit snug over his muscular legs. The corner of his mouth was tilted up as he perused the sketches.

Genevieve's heart raced. *Who is he? I know him from somewhere. Oh, gosh, I hope he's not someone I knew with Ed.* Many of those memories were blurred. Some she deliberately buried in the recesses of her mind. Would she even recognize anyone from that time when she was mostly under the influence of an illegal substance? She glanced over her shoulder, her stomach twisted in knots as with the realization she was too far from the exit to leave without causing a scene.

"David!" At Tricia's greeting, the man turned around. His ocean-blue eyes latched onto Genevieve and a brief frown creased his brow before he turned to Tricia. *He was at the prison chapel. The one I ran out on. What is he doing here? And why is he wearing long sleeves when it's so humid?* Genevieve's face warmed. Taking a step backwards, she fanned her face with a brochure and shifted her gaze around the room.

"David, I'd like you to meet Genevieve Trehearn. Gen, this is David Molineaux."

"Pleased to meet you, Genevieve." Her head snapped around at the sound of his warm voice. His soft smile revealed a dimple in his left cheek. Genevieve hesitated before shaking his hand. She hadn't touched another man since Ed, and she certainly wasn't used to such a gentle manner.

A jolt shot up her arm as their hands connected. She gasped and quickly pulled away, surprised by the warmth of his touch. Tricia

74

leaned forward and whispered something in David's ear, to which he glanced at Genevieve and nodded. Genevieve offered a half-smile as she clenched her fingers around her purse and shifted awkwardly on the polished timber floor.

A hush descended over the room as the emcee for the evening, a friend of Tom and Tricia's, spoke into a microphone set on a low-rise dais. "Ladies and gentlemen, if I can ask you to please take a seat, we'll get the evening under way."

Tricia linked her hand through Genevieve's arm again as she guided her to a table near the middle of the room. Tom approached and sat next to Tricia. Another couple, who Tricia introduced as the McGrath's, soon joined them.

"Anyone sitting here?" Genevieve glanced up at the deep voice. Warmth spread up her neck as her eyes connected with David's. Fiddling with the paper napkin on her lap, she shook her head.

"David!" Tricia exclaimed. "Please join us. It will be good to have someone else to help bring down the average age at the table!" Tom's roar of laughter ricocheted around the group.

With a grin that revealed his dimple, David shook out his napkin and laid it across his lap, his elbow brushing against Genevieve's arm. Startled by the warmth flooding over her, Genevieve angled her shoulders towards Tricia.

Breathe, Gen. Just breathe. It's probably just a natural reaction after not being close to another man for so long.

Tricia placed her hand on Genevieve's arm and leaned over. "I told David you were in jail. I hope you don't mind." Genevieve inhaled sharply. "He recognized you from his visit there a few weeks ago and asked. He doesn't know anything else. But I just thought you should know. You can relax a little. He's not going to bite." She smiled warmly as Genevieve toyed with the handle of the fork at her place setting.

Great. Now he's going to run the other way. She was thankful Tricia could run interference, but she wouldn't be there all the time. Was this how her future would play out? The awkward, trepidation wondering how people would react when they found out she had been in prison?

❧ 21 ❧

Grace was said, an announcement was made about the auction, and people settled into their seats as trays of food – a mixed variety of h'ors d'eurves, mini pastries and quiches - were placed around the tables.

"Tricia tells me you're an artist." David's voice melted over her and drew her thoughts away from how best to eat the vegetable quiche on her plate.

"Oh, I wouldn't say that." She cast him a sideways glance before returning her focus back to the food.

"From what I've seen, you've got quite a gift."

Her cheeks warmed at his words. "Thanks."

"Actually, your work looks familiar." David wiped the corner of his mouth with his napkin. Genevieve frowned, eyeing him curiously. He wasn't as good-looking as Ed – his nose was a little crooked, his hair a little too long - but he carried an air of humility and genuineness, rather than being egocentric or brash.

Genevieve's eyes travelled the length of his arm to his hand, wrapped around the glass of water on the table where his thumb tapped in time to the music. Scars marked his tanned skin, showing that he wasn't afraid of hard work.

"I'm not sure how. Tricia suggested I donate some of my drawings for the fundraiser, and that's the only place I've shown them." Genevieve was confused.

"My sister, Katy," David cleared his throat before taking a drink of water. "She gave me a drawing that looks to be of a similar style. A portrait of her, actually."

Genevieve's eyes widened. Her heart hammered against her chest. Reaching for her glass of water, she gulped the cool liquid. "Excuse me." Shakily, she set the glass on the table, splashing some onto the tablecloth as she pushed back her chair.

"Gen?" Tricia's voice was distant through the ringing in her ears. Sweat broke out on her forehead and suddenly, her summer dress seemed too warm in the stifling room. She needed to get outside into the fresh air.

Bumping a few chairs, she stumbled towards the back of the room. "Excuse me. I'm sorry." *Just get to the door. I need to get away from here. This is crazy. I can't deal with this. I just want to get away.*

Tears burned her eyes as she pushed through the door and stepped foot onto the concrete path. The scent of jasmine floated on the warm breeze. Night birds chorused in the dusk. Resting her hands on her knees, Genevieve drew in some deep breaths.

"Are you okay?" *David? Why on earth is he here?*

Genevieve quickly wiped her eyes. Light from inside the church hall cast shadows across the path. She nodded, her mouth dry.

"I'm sorry if I said something to upset you." He stood with one hand in the pocket of his jeans.

"No, you didn't say anything wrong." Genevieve didn't recognize the hoarse whisper coming from her mouth. Crossing her arms, she leaned against the brick wall, still warm from the afternoon sun. "I'm ..." What could she say? She'd been dreading this moment ever since she'd stepped foot outside the razor wire and into her freedom. She sighed. As with everything, the first time acknowledging her imprisonment would be the hardest. Surely it would get easier each time. "I may know your sister."

"Oh?" It was David's turn to look confused.

Genevieve traced the edge of her sandal along the cracks in the path. "Katy – Kaitlin? She's ... in prison, right?"

"Yeah, that's right." David nodded, his voice containing a hint of sadness.

"That's where I gave it to her." She turned her head, gazing out across the neatly mown lawn of the church property, allowing her words to hang in the air.

"Tricia told me you were in jail. And I saw you there when I visited a few weeks ago."

He remembered? With a soft chuckle, she shook her head. "Wow. Well, I'm glad we've cleared that up then. No sense in me trying to hide my criminal past. You knew all along?"

He nodded, his eyes full of empathy.

"So, I just had an anxiety attack for no reason?" She laughed and then sobered. "You haven't run away yet."

A smirk turned up the corner of his lips. "Why would I run away?"

"You don't know what I've done. I'm standing here, a free woman, but who's to say I can be trusted?" She was being snide, she knew. But she was testing the waters, to get an honest response.

"I trust Tricia's judgment," David said simply.

Wow. Just wow. Who is this guy? Such simple words, and yet they spoke volumes about his character.

"I'm sorry," Genevieve said, waving a hand around. "I'm just ... this is all new for me, and I'm scared people are going to judge me and run away."

David held his hands up as a coy grin slid across his mouth. "Not going to happen here."

Warmth infused Genevieve and she wrapped her arms around her waist to calm the flutter of nerves in her stomach. What could she say to that?

Taking a deep breath, she straightened her shoulders and held out her hand. "I'm Genevieve. I've just been released from jail."

David stepped forward, taking her hand. "Hi Genevieve. I'm David. My sister's in jail, and I wasn't that far off going myself." Genevieve stared at him, her mouth partly open.

"But that's a story for another day." He grinned, releasing her hand. "Shall we go back inside? Someone with an incredible talent has some sketches up for auction. I'm curious to see how much they raise."

David pushed through the doors of his local coffee shop with a long black in his keep-cup. After not being able to sleep well for the past few nights, fatigue wrapped around him like a heavy cloak, and the caffeine fix was a necessity to keep him functioning.

Ever since meeting Genevieve at Tom and Tricia's church fundraiser, the shy brunette had occupied his thoughts. He still couldn't believe she knew his sister, and that he owned one of her sketches.

HIS THOUGHTS TURNED TO THE NOTICE BOARD IN THE SPARE bedroom he'd converted to a home office. The creased ivory paper pinned to the board captured his attention every time he looked at it – the soulful look in his sister's eyes, the freckles sprinkled across her nose, the way her top lip curved more on one side - Genevieve had captured Katy's essence perfectly. The picture had distracted him to the point where he'd laced up his joggers and gone for a run late at night, because he couldn't get Genevieve out of his mind, which was crazy, as he'd just met her.

He'd done little work at home, and spent the last few nights flicking mindlessly through the television channels. He'd even been distracted during the sermon on Sunday night.

What had she done to serve time? His curiosity piqued. She looked harmless enough. Obviously Tricia and Tom saw something in her, or they wouldn't have opened their home so willingly. He longed to know what crime she'd committed to land in jail – if only to satisfy his own curiosity and reassure himself that she was trustworthy.

AFTER DRIVING THROUGH EARLY MORNING PEAK HOUR TRAFFIC, David pulled into the parking lot of Elevation Adventures. Unlocking the building and setting his coffee on his paper-strewn desk, he went through the usual routine of planning for the day.

Friday morning would see Tom and Tricia bringing over their group of women. If they were anything like Genevieve, he had nothing to worry about. *Would she be with them?* Excitement coiled in his belly at the thought of seeing her again. *Stop it, Dave. Focus.*

"Morning." Brett slid open the glass door and walked into the office. He tossed a plastic-wrapped blueberry muffin onto David's desk. "Two-for-one at the servo. You're first here, you win."

David laughed. "Thanks man." He peeled the wrap off and tossed it into the bin.

"What's up first today?" Brett draped his canvas satchel over the back of his chair and flicked on the computer.

Tapping a pen on the desk , David swivelled side-to-side in his chair. "We've got a kayaking group that Libby and Simon are taking out. I'm going to do some inventory. And you've got a climb just after lunch."

Brett leaned back and placed his hands behind his head. "Sounds good. Are you all set for Friday? Are you nervous?"

David tented his fingers against his mouth. "A little. I've got a few waivers to finalize today and then I'll sort the gear tomorrow."

"I hope it works out. I hope they don't do something stupid or try some weird move on you."

David chuckled and took a bite of the muffin. Blueberry juice squirted into his mouth as his teeth sank into the softness. "They'll be fine. I trust Tom and Tricia. I don't think I'll be getting any hardened criminals in the mix."

I'm standing here, a free woman, but who's to say I can be trusted? Genevieve's words came back to him. *What had she done to land in jail? Could she be trusted? God, help me to shake off my concerns. I pray you'll keep us safe and use me as you will.*

Sweeping the crumbs into a pile on his desk, he silently berated himself. Of course Genevieve could be trusted. In the short time he'd known Tom and Tricia, he was certain of their integrity and trusted them. They wouldn't suggest anything to jeopardise him or the company.

"Are you alright, man?" Brett leaned forward and eyed him across the room. "You look a bit lost there."

David popped the last morsel of muffin into his mouth and grinned. "I'm all good. Just have a few things on my mind at the moment." He turned to his computer and opened up the day's bookings. He printed off the paperwork required for the stock inventory and the waivers for Friday's outing.

Brett switched on the radio, and soon the sounds from one of the local rock stations filled the room. Brett tapped his pen on the desk in time with the beat and lip-synced to the well-known classic.

"You missed your calling." David chuckled, shaking his head. He loved working here. It was hard to believe God had taken the pieces of his broken life and used them for something good. Downing the last of his lukewarm coffee, he only hoped he could somehow be instrumental in offering the same to the women on Friday.

❧ 23 ❧

Genevieve darkened the lines on the cream-coloured paper. Using her fingers, she smudged the darkened area, softening the shadows across the face staring back at her.

The afternoon sun beat down, warming her bare arms as she sat on the front porch of the granny flat. The smell of freshly cut grass filled the air. And splashes and giggles from the neighbour's swimming pool reminded her that summer had well and truly arrived.

"Gen!" Tricia raised her hand as she made her way across the back-yard. She closed her notebook, hiding her current sketch. What started out as simple lines, soon progressed into soulful eyes, a dimple and a slightly off-centre nose. She hadn't meant to draw anyone in particular, but the likeness between her sketch and David was striking, and she certainly didn't want Tricia raising any eyebrows.

"Any luck with your applications?" Tricia stepped up onto the porch and leaned against the railing. She wore purple and silver rimmed glasses today. Genevieve loved the older woman's penchant for fashion-able accessories.

"I've had one response, asking for an interview Monday." It was one response more than she'd expected when she sent off her resumes to some nearby hair salons. It was a cheap franchise salon, offering clients the basics - a hair cut and blow dry. No fancy styling. No foils or colours. It was bottom of the rung, entry-level hairdressing. But, given her most recent work experience, it was better than nothing.

Tricia grinned. "Oh, that's great! I'll be praying for you." She tapped her fingers lightly on the wooden ledge, her silver bangles jingling on her wrist. "You're doing really well, Gen. How do you feel? I mean, you've only been out a short while, but you seem to be handling everything well so far."

"I feel okay. I had that little breakdown last week at the church fundraiser. I'm a little anxious about the interview, but I've got to learn to trust God, right?" She looked at Tricia for reassurance. This faith and trust thing was still all so new. But given her circumstances, she had no other option than to trust in God.

Smiling warmly, Tricia nodded. "He will take care of you. You may not always see God's hand at work, but He is always working in our lives in ways that we may never understand."

Genevieve nodded her understanding. She'd experienced that already. Just little coincidences – her friendship with Karina, Katy being David's sister, the gorgeous granny flat Tom and Tricia had generously allowed her to call home, and how they'd taken her under their wings, but given her enough freedom to learn to fly on her own.

Looking across the yard, Tricia tapped a finger on her lips. "I'm sure some of the ladies at church would love for you to cut their hair. I'll ask around for you."

"Thanks, Tricia. You don't have to do that. I'll see how I go with the interview and let you know."

Tricia pushed away from the railing. "A few people have asked about your drawings too, and are wondering if you would do some for them? All paid of course."

A smile made its way across Genevieve's face. "Really?" She placed one hand over her notebook, running her finger along the metal spiral on the spine. "I would like that."

"Great! I'll pass your details on."

Tears filled Genevieve's eyes as she thanked her older friend.

Tricia stepped forward and cupped Genevieve's cheek. "You are more than welcome, sweetheart." Genevieve swallowed the burn in her throat. Her mother had never shown her such tenderness or generosity.

"Oh, I almost forgot. That was my whole reason coming out to see you." She slapped her hand against her forehead. "This is what happens when you get old!" Genevieve laughed.

"Tom and I are taking a group of women, ex-prisoners, out kayaking on Friday morning. Would you like to join us?"

Ex-prisoners? Who are they? I wonder what their story is. Her heart began to race. That's what she was now. No matter how hard she tried to ignore the label, she couldn't hide from her past. The blemish would stay with her forever. She swallowed hard. The thought of associating with other prisoners outside the security of the razor wire frightened her.

"Tom and I know all the women personally, from our time visiting them in the prison and following up with them outside. They've done time for ..." Tricia paused and tilted her head. "Nothing that would endanger anyone now, let's put it that way."

Rolling a pencil between her fingers, Genevieve considered Tricia's words. Perhaps they'd made the same stupid mistakes she'd made, and were struggling with the same challenges and insecurities that she was. Surely they wouldn't be hardened criminals. She opened her mouth to say she'd think about it, but really, there was nothing to think about. She would go. She wasn't better than anyone else. Her fall from grace proved that.

Tom and Tricia had been overly generous in helping her adjust to life outside of prison, the least she could do would be to support them. Besides, it would be a good opportunity to meet other women and try something different.

"Count me in. It sounds like fun."

✵ 24 ✵

"Alright, ladies." Tom clapped his hands, gaining the attention of the six women mingling near the white minivan parked outside Penninsula Community Church. "Let's get going."

The women piled into the van, followed by Tricia, while Tom slid into the driver's seat.

Genevieve wiped her hands over her denim shorts and looked out the window as Tom shifted the bus into gear and drove out onto the road. Tricia turned around from her seat in the front row. "Seeing as we'll be spending the morning together, let's all introduce ourselves. I'm Tricia, as you all know." She smiled broadly and nodded encouragingly to Genevieve.

Clearing her throat, Genevieve gave a small wave as she introduced herself. The rest of the names were a blur, but she recalled a Justine, a Fiona and a Tessa among the group. Settling back against her seat, Genevieve gazed out the window as the scenery flew by.

Surprisingly, the women looked ... normal. To the passing eye, they could have been any women's group off on an outing, not a group of women with histories they'd rather forget. There were no prison greens, no standard issue running shoes, no greasy hair. To look at each of the women, one would assume they were a bunch of friends, perhaps work colleagues, heading out for a morning of fun.

Familiar landmarks soon came into view and Genevieve's stomach lurched with memories of a time she'd rather forget. South Bank was alive with splashes of colour and people out enjoying the warmer weather. The Ferris wheel stood tall and proud as it rotated against the backdrop of the city skyline. People swam in the man-made lagoon, while others sunbathed on the white sand of the beach.

The concrete buildings of the university across the river took her right back to her days of studying. In some ways she missed the challenge of the books, the pressure of exams and the pride in telling people she was undertaking a double degree. But, in astonishment, she realized she had never felt as free as she did now. She was free from the constraints of expectations others placed on her – her parents, Ed, and even herself. For the first time in her life, she was truly free to be herself.

"Here we are," Tom announced, pulling the minivan to a stop in front of a shipping container that had been painted dark blue. The company's logo was painted in white, blue and green across one corner of the building.

Tom stepped down from the drivers seat, opened the side door and stood to the side as the women filed out of the van and lingered uncertainly on the gravel parking lot.

The front door of the building slid open. A tall, sandy-blonde haired man stepped out and strode over to Tom.

"I'm Brett." He introduced himself, shaking Tom's hand firmly. "And you already know Dave."

Genevieve craned her neck to see the man stepping out of the building. He had a blue cap, matching the shade of the building, and sunglasses. Her breath hitched. *David? Really?* She lowered her eyes to the ground willing it to open up and swallow her whole.

The three men spent a few moments in discussion, while Tricia rallied the women around her.

"Has anyone kayaked before?"

One girl had, while everyone else shook their heads. "A long time ago," Genevieve murmured. She cast her eyes beyond the van, glimpsing the river through the trees, and shoved aside memories of halcyon days in the sun.

Brett assembled the group and gave them a short talk about safety, the use of life jackets and the basics of kayaking before handing them each an oar.

The woman who'd kayaked previously, paired up with Tessa.

Tom and Tricia paired up together. Brett went with Justine, leaving Fiona and her friend, and Genevieve and David.

"Hi. I didn't realize you were coming today." David carried a kayak over to Genevieve.

"I didn't realize you worked here," she replied, clutching the oar.

He adjusted his cap and grinned sheepishly. "I guess it's a surprise for both of us then. Do you want to grab the handle and help me carry it down to the water?" Genevieve nodded, and the pair edged the kayak through the trees down the slight embankment towards the river.

At the water's edge, Brett briefed everyone on the direction they would take.

David steadied the craft in knee-deep water as Genevieve climbed in. As David followed behind, the kayak rocked precariously and Genevieve gripped the sides. A deep laugh arose from behind her. "We're not going to tip. Not yet anyway."

Genevieve glanced over her shoulder and giggled. Bending her knees, she adjusted her hand position on the oar, trying to distract herself from David's close proximity. Hints of his spicy cologne wafted past, and with his tanned and muscular legs resting beside her hips, her body was on high alert.

"Ready?"

She nodded. On David's instruction, she lowered the oar into the water, dragging the blade towards her. White-knuckled, she gripped the handle, hoping the oar wouldn't slip into the water. Or worse, that she would cause them to capsize.

If only she was with someone other than David. Why had he chosen her for his partner? Surely one of the other women would be more suited. He sparked something completely unfamiliar in her. Her attraction to Ed had been nothing like the way David drew her in.

Should I talk to him? Or should I just focus on what I'm supposed to be doing? Everyone else seemed to be happily conversing as they rowed on the river.

"It's a nice day to be on the water." Genevieve twisted her torso and shoulders as Brett had instructed them to.

"It's beautiful," David replied. "Couldn't have asked for better weather."

Tick. That's the weather done. Now what?

"How long have you worked here?" The noise of heavy traffic almost drowned out her words as they rowed underneath the motorway.

"A little over five years."

"What did you do before that?"

The sound of traffic, the splashing of water, and conversation from the other craft surrounded them. Genevieve frowned. Had he not heard?

"What ..." she began again.

"I did a few things," David replied tersely, his tone silencing Genevieve.

Right. Well, that's that then. He obviously doesn't want to talk. Just keep your eyes ahead and focus on rowing.

The silence was excruciating as they made their way along the river, following behind the other craft. *What a stupid idea this was. Why am I stuck with him? I just asked him a simple question. He didn't need to be so rude.*

"Hold your oar up," David instructed as they neared a clearing off to the left. "I'm going to hop out and bring you into shore."

"Do you want me to get out here?"

"No, you stay there. I'll jump out."

Genevieve lifted her oar and placed it across her lap, water dripping down the handle onto her legs. The splash of David entering the water, and the rocking of the kayak made her grip the sides once more. She would not fall out and humiliate herself in front of him.

"You're not going to fall out." He grinned as he drew up beside her, gripping the craft and masterfully steering it to shore. She stiffened and tilted her chin. *What's his problem? Why did he brush me off before, and now act as if nothing happened? Stop it, Gen. You don't know the guy. There's no point getting worked up over nothing.*

Genevieve set the oar down and jumped out as soon as the sand gripped the hull of the craft. Briskly, she strode up the small beach area towards the rest of the group.

Brett and David spread some picnic rugs on the ground, and set out a mix of sandwiches, fruit, muffins and bottles of water.

"This is wonderful!" Tricia exclaimed, sweeping her hand across the generous spread.

"It's all part of our service," Brett grinned, tossing some grapes into his mouth.

Soon, the sun's warmth, the laughter between newfound friends, and the delicious food, made Genevieve forget about her qualm with David. If he didn't want to talk to her, that was fine. It was none of her business anyway. He was their host, and she was a guest.

After lunch, a couple of the women lay down on the picnic rugs, soaking in the sun's rays and enjoying the relaxing atmosphere. A few ventured out for a swim in the river, while Tom and Brett conversed near the kayaks.

Genevieve found a shaded spot away from the rest of the group and sat down. Memories flooded back as she cast her gaze across the river. Her classes in the lecture halls of the university on the opposite banks of the river. Swimming at the beach with Ed and some of their friends. Afternoon picnics at New Farm Park just around the river's bend. Tears stung her eyes as the pain of loss and humiliation washed over her.

God, I know I'm in a better place now, but it still hurts. I thought I had it good back then, but I really didn't. Perhaps all the pain was meant to be, because I feel peaceful for the first time in my life. I don't have much to show for my life, and I don't know what the future holds for me, but I know that I'm learning to trust you for that.

A shadow blocked the sun behind her. Despite the subtle drop in temperature, her body warmed and sensed his presence before he even moved into her line of sight.

"I'll probably cop a word or two from Brett for fraternizing with our guests, but it's not like it's the first time we've met." David grinned as he settled onto the sand beside her.

Genevieve glanced his way, shielding her eyes from the sun.

"I just thought you might want some company, all over here on your own."

"I'm good," she replied, looking across at the other women laughing and splashing in the water. She didn't mind being alone. It afforded her plenty of time to think and reflect on her life.

"Look, I didn't mean to sound rude when you asked me what I did prior to this job." David linked his hands together over his knees. His sunglasses shielded his eyes, but Genevieve guessed he was looking out across the water.

"It's all good. You don't have to tell me." She didn't mean to sound defensive. It was her natural armour of self-preservation against people she didn't yet know how to trust.

"You're right. I don't have to. But ..." A large sigh filled the space between them. Genevieve glanced his way.

Further along the shore, Tom and Brett were packing up the picnic. "I should go and help them." David glanced at his watch. "We'll need to get going soon." He pushed to his feet. "I'm probably out of line, but did you want to have dinner with me tonight?"

Genevieve straightened her back, looking up and down the beach. "Do you ask all your guests out for dinner?" Her lips twitched and her heart raced. It had been a long time since someone asked her out.

David adjusted his cap. "No. Just the one I'd like to get to know a little more."

She inspected her nails closely. "Um ... sure."

"Great," David replied warmly. "I finish at five. Shall I pick you up at six?"

"Okay," Genevieve squeaked. David held out his hand and pulled her to standing. She gave a nervous laugh as she almost collided with his chest. Stepping away, she quickly brushed the sand off her shorts and made her way back to the kayak.

The trip back to the warehouse was quiet. Genevieve's skin was flushed – whether from the sun or knowing that David was right behind her – she couldn't be sure. Overwhelm slammed into her. *Is this a date? Don't think of it as a date. Think of him as a new friend you're getting to know. No more. No less.*

25

David pulled to a stop outside Tom and Tricia's house. He drummed his palms on the steering wheel and exhaled. Brett had quizzed him once everyone had left the kayaking tour. Did he think it was wise to meet up with an ex-con? David gently informed him that he'd previously met Genevieve, and he implicitly trusted Tom and Tricia's judgment of character.

There was something beyond Genevieve's natural beauty that drew him in. The fact that she was an ex-con didn't bother him. What worried him was that *she* might run away once she found out about his sordid past.

Loosening the collar of his shirt, he stepped out of the ute and strode up to the front door, shoving the keys into the back pocket of his jeans.

Before he had a chance to knock, Tricia opened the screen door.

"Oh, David. I'm so happy that you've asked Gen out for dinner." She ushered David through the living room and out the back door. "She's a lovely girl, and she recently committed her life to Christ. I'm glad she's starting to make friends."

Friends. Right. Must keep that in check.

Tricia stepped up onto the porch of the granny flat and knocked on the door. "Gen, David's here!" David stood back, clasping his hands behind his back, suddenly feeling inadequate dressed in his dark blue denims and long sleeve black shirt. He had never been one for designer labels or spending a fortune on clothes. Comfortable and presentable were his style. Which was perhaps why he was now questioning the bland colours in his wardrobe.

As Genevieve opened the door and stepped out, a wave of peach and sandalwood slammed into him.

"H- Hi," he stammered.

"Hi." She smiled, adjusting the strap of her purse across her shoulder.

"Well," Tricia stepped back and gestured to the pair. "I'll let you two go and enjoy dinner. Any idea where you're going?"

David ran a hand across his jaw, his thoughts clouded by the delicious scent of her perfume and how stunning she looked in the simple yellow sundress floating around her legs.

"Um ... I was thinking the Thai restaurant down near the bay. That's if you like Thai?" He glanced at Genevieve. "Otherwise there are a few other places we can choose from."

"I love Thai food!" Genevieve exclaimed, her brown eyes sparkling gold in the last rays of sun as it dipped behind the main house.

"Well, off you go. Tom and I are just having a fish curry pie. It doesn't sound as tantalizing or exotic as Thai." She grinned and waved as David led Genevieve down the stairs and along the path around the side of the house.

His much-loved ute looked worse for wear as they approached, and he suddenly wished he'd asked Brett or Josh if he could borrow their car.

"Sorry about this pile of junk," he murmured, opening the door for Genevieve.

She waved her hand and slid onto the worn seat. "It goes, doesn't it?"

He nodded. *Just.*

"Then that's all a car needs to do."

Closing the door, he leaned against the back panel, pausing to catch his breath. He'd never used material possessions to impress a girl before, so why was the state of his vehicle bothering him so much? Then again, he'd never really tried to impress a girl before. His past followed him like a bad stench and had prevented him from pursuing any potential relationships.

By the time they arrived at the bayside restaurant, David's shoulders were tense and sweat trickled down his neck. He jumped out of the car, grateful to be out of the confines of the cab and away from the onslaught of Genevieve's sweet perfume. Wiping his palms on the front of his jeans, he scooted around opened Genevieve's door.

They chose a table outside overlooking a pond, complete with a fountain and goldfish swimming leisurely through the clear water. Lanterns hung around the perimeter of the dining area. Wind chimes tinkled in the breeze blowing off the ocean.

David toyed with the napkin on the table after they'd placed their orders. "Did you enjoy today?"

Genevieve glanced up and nodded, a warm smile lighting her face and her skin glowing in the soft lantern light. "I did. I had a great time, thank you."

"That's good. That's the first time we've ..." *Darn! Why bring up her imprisonment?*

She reached across the table, briefly covering her hand over his. David adjusted the collar around his neck, allowing the air to cool his skin.

"It's okay. You don't have to tread lightly. It's the truth - it's the first time you've taken women prisoners out on an adventure."

He gave a short laugh. "I'm sorry. I don't want to upset you."

Folding her hands on her lap, Genevieve lowered her eyes. "You're not going to upset me. I've only been out a few weeks, so I guess it's going to take me some time to get over it. I can't expect to just forget it. Besides, prison is always going to be a part of me, so I may as well own it. Right?"

She raised her chin, and their eyes collided in a torrent of under-standing.

"Right," he murmured, clasping his hands together and resting them under his chin. Where did they go from here? He wanted her to know he didn't care about her past. What she'd done, didn't matter. He liked her for who she was now.

A mix of pad Thai and curry dishes were placed before them. As they ate, David asked Genevieve about her art, if she'd found work and about her family. She eagerly answered a few questions, but was evasive about others. Sensing her family was a sensitive topic, he didn't press any further.

❦ 26 ❦

fter paying for their meal, David suggested a walk along the waterfront. Sea glass and shards of coral lay scattered across the sandy shore, and buoys bobbed up and down in the inky water.

"Do you have family nearby?"

Genevieve gathered her dress against the breeze, while David led the way across some rocks to sit down. Water lapped rhythmically against the rocks below. Lights from the Port of Brisbane – where cargo ships arrived with their wares - glimmered further along the coastline. On the left, the jetty stretched out into the ocean, its white pillars contrasting against the dark water.

"Katy's in jail, as you know. My Dad died when I was young. And my Mum," he sighed, looping his fingers across his knees. "She's still out on the family farm."

"Do you see her much?" Genevieve's arm brushed against his shirt as she tried to find a comfortable position.

"No, I don't. I've had to set some boundaries when it comes to my relationship with my mother."

"I get that," Genevieve whispered, tucking flyaway strands of hair behind her ear. David's heart pounded. *Lord, I don't want to scare her away. Does she need to know everything?*

Gazing out across the dark ocean, he swallowed the heaviness building in his chest. Moonlight shone a silver path across the rippled surface. "It's my fault Katy's in jail," he murmured, waiting for Genevieve's gasp of surprise. But it never came. Instead, she raised an eyebrow and waited for him to continue. So he did.

For only the second time in his life, he poured out his heart – detailing the drugs, the alcohol, how he'd let his sister down because he was in such a bad way, the rejection and lack of concern from their mother, the different men who'd been their pseudo-father. He told her about his time living on the streets, shooting up and too stoned to care what happened to him or anyone else. He'd been on rock bottom, lower than scum. But someone introduced him to Robert, who invited him on a hike with Elevation Adventures, and then introduced him to Jesus. *That* was the turning point in his life.

Tears burned his eyes and his shoulders relaxed, releasing the burden of shame he'd carried for too long.

"Thank you for telling me." Genevieve covered his hand with her own and gave a light squeeze.

"We've got a similar story," she said, extracting her hand and running it over the seam on her dress. "Except I *did* end up in jail. Which I'm now learning, as difficult as it is to accept, was a good thing."

"What about your family?" David turned his head, longing to run his finger along her cheek. Her skin glowed with the after effects of a day spent in the sun.

"I haven't seen them since I was sentenced." She shrugged dispassionately as she gazed out across the moonlit water. "I sometimes wonder if I should contact them, but I'm scared of what will happen. Not that they can do anything to hurt me. They've already done that." She laughed abruptly.

David's stomach clenched as his own memories flooded back. He knew the bitterness of rejection that lay just beneath the surface. He knew the disappointment of being let down by those who were supposed to love you unconditionally.

"I haven't spoken to my mother in years," David murmured. It had been his mother's choice. He had contacted her time and again, but not once did she bother reciprocating. It still hurt at times, but God had helped him forgive when it was the last thing he wanted to do. *He wasn't to blame for her actions.* All he could do was offer forgiveness, in the same way God had forgiven him for all his misdeeds. "Could you write to your parents?"

"Maybe." Genevieve swung her legs back and forth over the edge of the rocks. "So, why do you wear long sleeves all the time?"

David frowned at the sudden change in topic. *Where did that come from?* He tugged at his sleeves and drew in a sharp breath. *Here goes. It's all or nothing.* With the water lapping quietly against the rocks, and a cool breeze blowing in off the ocean, David slowly pushed his sleeves up and held his arms out for Genevieve to see.

Moonlight shone across the black ink covering his forearms. Symbols of rebellion and a constant reminder of choices he'd made back when drugs had distorted his mind. He rolled his arms over, revealing thick track marks scarring the skin where the ink couldn't touch.

Goosebumps erupted as Genevieve lightly traced her fingers over the intricate patterns of the tattoos and then across his scars. Her unspoken words and her gentle touch penetrating through the walls of his heart.

"This is why." His voice, barely above a whisper, trembled. His work colleagues had seen some of his tattoos, but he always covered his arms – wanting to present a professional image to the people he took out on tours. Likewise with his friends at church. No one had been close enough to discover the scars of his past.

"It's nothing to be ashamed of." Not only her touch, but also her words, were soft and genuine, weaving their way into the crevices of his heart. "They are a part of you. A reminder of what you've been through, and how far you've come."

David's eyes burned. Words escaped him. She was struggling with her own worth, and yet she had enough compassion to pour out for him.

The sound of a foghorn blasted in the distance. Lights from a cargo ship drifted across the horizon. And the lingering scent of Genevieve's perfume mingled with the salty air, filling David's senses.

Genevieve edged closer on the rock and looped her hand through his arm. She rested her head on his shoulder, her hair tickling his neck. With her other hand, she traced over the markings on his arm.

"Thank you for showing me. To healing and new beginnings," she whispered.

27

Sleep evaded her. Genevieve tossed and turned, kicking the bed covers off, and then pulling them back up when she became too cold. The evening with David had been wonderful. They'd connected on a deep level, and yet she remained guarded. She'd been quick to fall in love with Ed, and look where that had landed her. She didn't want to repeat past mistakes.

Could you write to your parents? David's suggestion floated through her thoughts. For years, she'd wanted to reach out to them, but shame, embarrassment and fear held her back. She'd let them down and she didn't want them to remind her of her failures. But, if she was going to move forward with her life, she needed to address the relationship with them, as uncomfortable as it may be.

Do they still live on Hamilton Hill? Of course they would. I can't imagine Mum wanting to move anywhere else unless it had a ridiculous price tag attached.

Glancing at the numbers illuminated on the clock beside her bed, Genevieve sighed and pushed back the covers. Padding across the room, she flicked on the lamp and sat down at the table. Opening a lined notepad, she gripped her pen above the blank page.

It's now or never. God, you tell us to forgive those who hurt us. I've been carrying around this hurt and anger towards my parents for so long, and I need you to take it from me. If they don't want me in their lives, that's fine, help me to deal with that. You are all I need. I pray that you'll help me to forgive them.

In the dim glow of the lamp, Genevieve held pen to paper and began writing. She poured out her hurt, apologized for hurting them and asked for their forgiveness. The ink ran as tears splashed onto the paper. Even if her parents didn't respond, she felt a release from years of self-loathing and resentment towards them. Her past was in the past. Her parents made their own choices, just like she'd made the decisions that landed her in jail. It was time to put the shame of her past behind her and embrace the future.

❧ 28 ❧

"Here." David tossed Genevieve a pair of fingerless cowhide leather gloves. She finished pulling on her shoes and snatched the gloves from the air. Slipping them over her fingers, she grabbed the ropes and harnesses out of the ute and followed David along the path towards the base of the cliff.

"Nervous?" He grinned. Metal clips clanged against each other as they dropped the equipment on the ground.

"A little." With one hand on her hip, she shielded her eyes and arched her neck as she gazed up the steep grey rock face. Climbing hooks jutted out at various intervals. Shaking her head, Genevieve stepped into a harness and adjusted the straps over her full-length gym pants.

"You know this isn't a good look, right?"

David chuckled. "Trust me, I've seen a lot worse." Genevieve laughed and playfully thumped David on the arm.

The past few weeks had seen them exploring a lot of what Brisbane and its surrounds had to offer. From the rainforest to the river, and sharing many sunrises together, Genevieve found herself falling in love with the outdoors.

Gone were the nights of drinking wine at a fancy bar, or dancing until the early hours of dawn. Those cheap thrills were long gone. No drug or alcohol-induced high could compare to the adrenaline rush she got from hiking in The Glasshouse Mountain ranges, or along suburban tracks. They'd spent many Sunday afternoons kayaking along the river and picnicking in leafy alcoves, before heading back and going to church. But this was the first time she was attempting to rock climb.

"I didn't realize it was quite so big. It doesn't look so ominous from the other side of the river!" Genevieve clipped the straps of her helmet together under her chin.

"Yep. That's what makes it so great for climbing." David stepped over and clipped the carabiner to her harness.

"Remember, keep your hips close to the rock. Use your legs to push, not your arms, and rest when you feel like it."

Genevieve licked her dry lips and nodded. She puffed out a breath of air, willing her nerves to settle. Turning, she grabbed David, pressing her fingers into his forearms. "Don't let me fall."

"I'm not going to. If you slip, I've got you." He held up the ropes attached to her harness. Leaning down, he brushed his lips against her cheek and stepped back, grinning.

She stood, her mouth agape, her skin tingling.

"You'll be fine, Gen." She nodded, distracted by the delicate sensation of his lips on her cheek.

"Remember, hand, foot, hand, foot. Rest when you need to. There's no rush."

Walking over to the wall, Genevieve closed her eyes and rolled her shoulders. Resting her hand on the warm rock, she uttered a quick prayer. *Right. I can do this. I can do this, and I won't fall and make a fool of myself.*

Tentatively, she lifted one hand and felt along the wall until she found a comfortable grip. Pushing with her legs, she raised one foot and placed it on a small ledge a little way off the ground. She moved her other hand, finding another crevice to cling to. She did the same with her remaining foot. Pressing herself against the rock face, she breathed a sigh of relief. She was off the ground!

"Great job!" David enthused. Sweat beaded on her brow and trickled between her shoulder blades as the sun lowered across the city. Her breathing became harder and her arms ached. But the adrenaline pulsing through her veins made her feel alive.

Her hand reached up to find another ledge to grip. She still had a long way to go to reach the top. It wouldn't happen today, not on her first climb. Genevieve turned her head, eyeing the other climbers adeptly scaling the cliff. Suddenly, her foot slipped and her body slammed against the rock. Pain jolted down her side as jagged edges of rock pierced her skin. Grasping the rope with sheer strength, she rapidly blinked away the tears blurring her vision.

"Grab a ledge if you can." David's calm voice carried up as she swung against the rock once more.

"Lean back in your harness."

"What?" Genevieve called over her shoulder as she worked her fingers into a small crevice.

"Put your legs out in front of you, and lean into your harness, like you're sitting down."

"Why?"

"It's the best way to bring you down. Push your legs against the wall and hold onto the rope."

Tentatively, Genevieve gripped the rope, feeling the burn through the gloves as it slid through her palms. She leaned back in the harness as David instructed, and ever so slowly, inched her way down the rock until her feet hit the ground.

Allowing the ropes to slacken, David stepped forward. "Are you alright?" He ran his fingers lightly over the grazes on her skin before his eyes met hers in concern.

"I'll be fine. My legs feel like jelly, but I'm sure they'll recover." Genevieve forced a smile as she unclipped her helmet and tightened her ponytail.

David rummaged through his backpack and produced a bottle of water and some gauze from a first aid kit. Soaking the gauze, he gently wiped over the open grazes on Genevieve's arm. As the wet material made contact with her wounded flesh, she inhaled sharply.

"Sorry," he murmured. "I just want to get any debris out of the cuts."

Pressing her lips together, Genevieve nodded and followed his fingers as they blazed a trail of warmth across her skin.

❧ 29 ❧

The sky glowed orange as the sun dipped behind the city skyline. The usually brown river was a ribbon of shimmering gold as it wound underneath bridges and between the city sights.

"That was great," Genevieve sighed, leaning her head against the seat as David drove onto the M1. Her arms smarted from her slip against the rock face, but the pain was worth it for the exhilaration of the climb.

"Glad you liked it." He shot a grin her way. "It's good fun."

"I still can't believe you get to do it for a job."

"I'm very blessed. All I can say is, God was looking out for me."

Genevieve tapped her fingers against her chin as she looked out the window. Cars sped by in the opposite direction. Billboards along the motorway advertised the latest theatre production. Street lights gradually flickered on as the sun's last rays disappeared.

"Do you want to pick up some dinner? My shout." David left the motorway and drove along the slip road.

"Sure." At Genevieve's suggestion, they found a drive-through, ordered some takeaway and continued on to David's house.

Carrying the paper bags with their meals, Genevieve followed David up the path to his front porch.

"This is nice." Genevieve eyed the simple furnishings as she followed David into the house and through the living room to the kitchen.

"If you like eighties interior design." David stepped out onto the back deck, placing the drinks on a square wooden table in the middle of the deck. Genevieve scooped their burgers and fries out of the paper bag before sitting down.

"It's homely. Comfortable."

David shrugged. "I guess. I'm not much of a homebody, so I don't really give much thought to anything other than what I need."

"That's a good way to be though." Something warm brushed against Genevieve's leg. She looked down as a black tail disappeared from sight.

"Oh, you're adorable."

"Thanks." David grinned and winked.

"Not you!" *Although, yes, you are quite adorable.* Mocking hurt, David placed his hands over his heart.

"The cat."

"Oh, BC. I haven't seen her in ages. I just leave food out and she comes and goes as she pleases."

"BC?" Placing a fry in her mouth, Genevieve tilted her head.

David finished his mouthful of burger. "Black Cat. Very unoriginal. I'm hopeless with names."

Genevieve threw her head back in laughter. "Black Cat? Gosh, I wouldn't want you naming my children!" Her eyes widened and heat flared over her face. *Did I just say that? Please hide me now.* Mortified, she grabbed a handful of fries and popped them in her mouth, looking around the deck for the cat, doing anything to avoid David's gaze. "Where did you go, little gal?" *Come back and save me from this humiliation!*

David chuckled. Her reaction was cute, and he wanted to reach over and tuck the loose strands of hair behind her ear. Instead, he pressed his fingers into his palms and averted his eyes.

"She's such a fickle creature. She only shows up when she wants something."

"That reminds me of people I used to know," Genevieve sighed, resting her elbows on the table. David eyed the brunette across from him, tracing the contours of her face as she gazed out over his backyard.

"Me too," he murmured.

Crickets chirped from somewhere in the garden. Moths fluttered around the naked bulb on the ceiling. A comfortable silence settled over them as they ate the remainder of their dinner.

"What are your plans, Gen?" David slurped his drink through the straw.

"What do you mean?"

"Do you think you'll try and study again?"

Genevieve ran her fingers over the edge of her burger wrapper. "I think study is completely out of the question for now. *Law* is completely out of the picture. I think it was more to please my parents than for the love of it. And look where that got me." She chuckled as her eyes roamed the outdoor space. There was nothing outstanding about David's outdoor area. But it was neat. A row of native ornamental plants bordered the back fence. A hammock was strung between two posts on the deck, and a scratching post for the cat stood near the back door.

"They'd be so proud of you if they could see you now," David murmured.

"You don't know my parents." Genevieve shot him an incredulous look. "I don't think they'd be proud of me unless I passed the bar exam and had a nameplate on an office door in George Street."

"Well, I'm proud of you." His face warmed under her scrutiny. Drumming his fingers on the table, he squared his jaw and returned her gaze. *All or nothing, Dave.* "I know it's not much consolation. I'm not your Mum or Dad. But I see the beautiful woman you've become, and the change God has made in your life. I see your heart full of kindness for those around you, your humility, and your yearning to make a difference in people's lives."

Genevieve's eyelids fluttered, and once again David was on the receiving end of her incredulity.

"David, I ... I don't know what to say."

Willing the rampant fluttering in his chest to subside, he reached across the table and wove his fingers through hers.

"You don't have to say anything," he whispered. "Just continue to shine."

❦ 30 ❧

"S o, how long have you had BC?" Genevieve tightened her ponytail and glanced at David as they exited the motorway. There were barely any other vehicles on the road due to the public holiday, which meant sleep-ins for most people, and an almost-deserted city.

"I should've asked you that last week when I was at your house, but I completely forgot." She covered a yawn as they crossed the river. They'd driven to the top of Mt Coot-tha to watch the spectacular sunrise over the city. It had been a blissful way to start the day.

"About four years." David's elbow rested on the window ledge. His fingers tapped on the steering wheel. "He was a stray my sister found before ..." A large sigh emanated from him.

"It's okay, David." Genevieve placed a hand over his. "You don't need to be ashamed or embarrassed with me. Remember?"

He gave a half-smile before shifting gears and slowing down for a corner. "Yeah, sorry. I'm not ashamed. It's just that ..." His voice trailed off. He needed to let go of the guilt over his part in Katy's incarceration. He hadn't made the choices for her.

"She's pretty lucky to have you." Genevieve settled against the worn cloth seat and smiled wistfully.

"Who are we talking about here? Katy or BC?"

"Both?" Genevieve's timid voice stirred something in his chest. Leaning his head back, he couldn't contain the grin spreading across his face.

GRAVEL CRUNCHED UNDER THE TYRES AS THEY PULLED INTO THE parking lot of Elevation Adventures a few minutes later.

"Should be a nice day out on the water." David adjusted his cap and held Genevieve's door open as she stepped out. Offering her thanks, she shrugged into her backpack and pulled her cap over her ponytail. David reached out and grabbed her hand, leading the way across the parking lot. Holding her hand felt so natural, and warmth infused him with the comfort of her companionship as they walked the short distance to the office.

"What the ...?" David stopped suddenly, causing Genevieve to bump into his side.

"What on earth?" She murmured, letting go of his hand as she slowly stepped towards the building. Graffiti tags, in black, red and white, covered the front and side walls of the office. David removed his cap and silently walked around the side of the building, perusing the extent of the damage. Genevieve dropped her backpack to the ground and wandered in the other direction, meeting up with David at the back of the building.

"There's nothing on that side." She pointed behind her. "And the windows are all in one piece."

"It's unbelievable." David shook his head, stunned by the vandalism. He strode over to the storage shed which appeared unscathed. The door was still locked, and there were no graffiti tags anywhere.

See, this is what happens when you try to help others. Someone's upset because you've taken on the less-than-desirables. You brought this upon yourself and the business. You knew something like this would happen, and sure enough, it has.

"David?" Genevieve's hand closed over his shoulder. Surveying the damage, he continued to shake his head.

"I knew this would happen," he muttered as he pulled away and unlocked the shed.

"You can't have known it would happen." Genevieve followed him inside where kayaks and paddle boards were stacked high on storage racks. Life jackets overflowed from some storage tubs against the far wall. And oars leaned together in a corner.

David swung around. Light filtering in through the windows cast a shadow over his face, magnifying the twitch in his jaw.

"I've been working with kids who are angry with the world. You know, I really thought I was getting through to them. Making a difference. And then, this." He sliced his hand through the air as he paced around the shed.

Genevieve folded her arms and waited for him to finish his tirade. "And then, I stupidly agreed to take on ex-cons. Who knows what they're capable of? I'm putting the business and my colleagues at risk."

Heat flared across Genevieve's face. Her skin prickled in irritation. How dare he try and blame the ex-prisoners? She may not know the women, but they all had something in common – they were all trying hard to put their past behind them and move on.

Tom and Tricia had been instrumental in helping her transition back into society. They had been considerate of her feelings, understanding of her fears, and encouraging with their words, and she knew others had experienced the same thing. How *dare* he throw all that progress away by insinuating any of the women did this to his property?

"Excuse me?" With hands on her hips, she strode over and stood right in front of him. Narrowing her eyes, she took some slow, deep breaths to calm herself down.

"What?" David looked up in surprise.

"That's all a bit harsh, isn't it?"

David's blank expression told her he had no clue what she was mad about.

"Blaming the kids or the women for the graffiti."

With a startled expression glancing his face, David took a step backwards. "I – I didn't mean ... " He lowered his head as realization dawned. "I'm sorry."

Genevieve's nostrils flared. There was so much she could say, but she didn't want to spout off words in anger. Moments passed as they eyed each other. David's sorrowful eyes squeezed her heart.

Finally, Genevieve broke the silence. "I'm going outside to wait."

"Gen ..." David took a few steps towards her, but she shook her head and continued out the door. She heard him hit the side of the building and angrily chide himself as she strode across the parking lot.

❧ 31 ❧

Hurt and confusion whirled within as Genevieve wandered through a clearing of trees and sat by the water. The damp sand seeped through her shorts.

Why is he being so rude? Perhaps I'm just being over-sensitive. But surely there was no need for him to accuse any of us for that mess. If one of the people she trusted implicitly made her feel vulnerable, then what chance was there of being accepted by everyone else?

She plucked a stalk of grass from the ground, twirling it through her fingers. Ants scurried haphazardly across the sand. A ferry chugged past on the river, while leaves rustled overhead in the light breeze blowing off the water. She shouldn't let one offhand comment get under her skin. But it had. She was extremely self-conscious of her past. And no matter how hard she tried, would always be there.

God, what am I to do? I really don't like this awful way I'm feeling. I'm hurt. I'm annoyed. And I don't want this to ruin the good thing we've got going.

Tears sprang in her eyes. Across the river, early morning joggers ran along the path winding past the botanical gardens. Footfall over leaf litter drew her attention and she glanced over her shoulder. Drawing her knees to her chest, she turned and continued looking at the water.

"Mind if I sit?"

Genevieve shook her head. The damp ground squelched as David sat with enough space between them for another person. "I'm really sorry for what I said back there." He looped his hands over his knees.

Genevieve remained silent, her mind a myriad of thoughts. Did he assume she wasn't trustworthy as well? Did her prison sentence tarnish her to the point where he was quick to cast blame?

"I was out of line." A large sigh drew Genevieve's attention. "It was completely insensitive of me."

Yes, it was. "I thought you enjoyed working with the kids and doing the outreach programs."

"I do. Sometimes they're hard work. Overall, they're great. But some of them can still be recalcitrant regardless of how much I try."

"You can only do so much. You can't change everyone."

"I wish I could." His words were quiet, barely audible over birdsong in the trees and the water lapping on the shore. "Can I be honest, Gen?"

She gave a short laugh. "Please do. I only want honest people in my life. I can't bear the thought of living with lies or half-truths." Her eyes outlined his profile, his throat bobbing up and down as he swallowed.

"I was scared about taking on the prisoner outreach program. I've seen how Tom and Tricia work with them, and they do an amazing job. I don't know why I was scared. I mean, my sister's in prison." Clenching his hands together, he tilted his chin and cast his eyes downstream. "I guess because I've seen and heard what goes on in there, and I felt vulnerable. I don't feel worthy to be leading these groups, and I've deflected my own insecurities onto people who deserve so much more grace than I can give. I've harboured a fear that someone will see that I'm no one special. And I guess I felt my fears came to fruition when I saw the graffiti."

Shaking her head, Genevieve stretched her legs out on the cool sand. "That's the stupidest thing I've ever heard."

"Pardon?" David flinched, leaning his body away as he eyed Genevieve.

"You don't really believe those lies, do you? You're the most qualified person I know who could take kids and ex-cons under their wing. You've been in their shoes. You know what it's like to hate the world and everyone in it. So what if Katy's in prison? No one's going to judge you for that. At least you know how to relate to the women in your program." She snapped off another blade of grass and ran her fingers along the edge. "I've got the same insecurities, David. I'm so worried people are going to find out about what I've done, and they're going to turn their backs on me."

Silence enveloped them. Genevieve's pulse pounded in her ears. *I've said too much. Now he's just going to stand up and walk away.*

"Thank you."

"For what?"

"Being open with me." David removed his cap and ran a hand through his hair. "I guess I've been trying to do things in my own strength, rather than rely on God. I've had a few people tell me similar things, so I'm guessing God's trying to get my attention. I just need to let go of my inadequacies and trust God."

A soft laugh floated from Genevieve's lips. "I guess we both do."

David edged closer, closing the gap between them. "I'm guessing you don't want to go out on the water anymore?"

Genevieve leaned back on her hands, digging her fingers into the moist sand. "Not today."

"Fair enough. I'm sorry I've ruined your day."

Genevieve pushed herself to standing, brushing the sand off her shorts and legs. "You haven't ruined my day. Come on." She reached down, offering David her hand. A flicker of confusion crossed his face as he hesitantly took her hand and stood.

"Where are we going?"

❧ 32 ❧

Without a word, Genevieve led David up the embankment and over to the storage shed. She released his hand and walked over to some metal shelving on the wall.

"What are you doing?"

"Getting some paint."

Folding his arms across his chest, David leaned against the doorway following Genevieve's every move. After scanning the shelves, Genevieve armed herself with brushes and two tins of paint, and made her way back to the office building.

"Can I borrow your keys?" She called over her shoulder as she set the tins and brushes on the ground.

"What are you doing?" David chuckled as he reached her. "Talk to me. Tell me what you're up to."

"I'm going to paint." With her hands on her hips, she surveyed the side wall.

"What? Why?"

With a sigh, turned to face David.

"I'm going to paint the walls of this building," she enunciated slowly, "because someone has made a mess of them. I'm going to clean it up by painting over the tags."

David's expression sobered and he reached out a hand. "You really don't have to do this, Gen."

Scuffing some pebbles along the ground, she shrugged. "I know. But I want to. So, if I could have your keys to open the tins, I would be most grateful."

AFTER OPENING THE TINS, GENEVIEVE PROMPTLY TOOK A BRUSH AND a tin of paint and walked around the side of the building. David stood rooted to the spot.

Unbelievable. She's actually going to do it. Well, I won't let her do it alone. He stooped down and grabbed the remaining tin and paintbrush. Moving to the front of the office, David slapped paint onto the metal structure, covering the ghastly graffiti. Minutes ticked by, and he settled into a good rhythm with the brush strokes.

Sweat trickled down his back as the sun beat down. The faint sounds of humming drifted around the side of the building. David paused and listened. The tune was a familiar chorus from church.

He quietly made his way to the corner and peered around. The muscles in Genevieve's arms rippled as she moved the brush smoothly over the building. She hummed as she worked, and her face exuded an incredible peace.

She's so beautiful. David's heart slammed against his ribs, and his breath caught as he watched, mesmerized by Genevieve's simple act of worship.

Suddenly, she glanced up. "How long have you been standing there?"

With a wry grin, David folded his arms. "Long enough to know you have a beautiful voice."

A flush spread over her neck and her eyes widened briefly, before she strode over.

"You've got something there." She pointed to David's face.

With the back of his sleeve, David wiped across his face. "Where?"

Before he could react, Genevieve whipped out the paintbrush and swiped it across his nose.

"There." With a smirk, she returned to her spot and continued spreading the dark blue paint over the graffiti.

David's mouth dropped open. His feet remained planted to the ground. Slowly, he wiped his fingers across his nose. Yes, there was definitely paint there.

Containing a laugh, he casually stepped over to her. Her eyes flicked towards him, but she continued painting and humming. When he was directly behind her, he reached out and grabbed her waist. Squeals filled the air as Genevieve tried to escape. The paintbrush fell to the ground, dirt and grass coating the paint-filled bristles. Genevieve's laughter rang out as she ducked and weaved, trying to escape David's tormenting fingers.

With both of them laughing and breathless, David captured Genevieve's arms, pulling her back against his chest. Slowly she turned to face him. Their breath intermingled and their eyes locked in a dance of longing and questioning. David slid his hands down and captured Genevieve's in his own. Leaning down he brushed his lips across hers.

In an instant, his world shifted, and his heart beat with a new rhythm – a promise of hope and a cascade of love for the woman standing before him.

Reluctantly, he released her hands and stepped away. "Sorry," he whispered. "I ..."

Reaching up, Genevieve cupped his cheek, her palm burning his skin. "Don't be." She smiled softly before turning to pick up the discarded paintbrush. David exhaled and closed his eyes, willing the pounding in his chest to slow.

After washing the paintbrushes out, Genevieve and David stood back to admire their work. Aside from a few red paint splatters, no one would know any different.

"Looks great. Thank you." And, as if it were the most natural thing in the world, David pulled Genevieve into his arms, and placed a lingering kiss on top of her head.

"Shall we take a rain check on the kayaking?"

EPILOGUE

Working in the dim lantern light, Genevieve shaded the contours of the face on the cream paper. The nose. The cheeks. The lips. Her breath caught with the uncanny likeness. She'd captured his passion so perfectly, and her heart welled with love. She placed the pencil down, satisfied with her efforts, and carefully rolled the paper up before sliding a rubber band over the top. She wouldn't show him just yet. Just like the other pictures she'd drawn of him, they were her own private treasures that captured the essence of her love's generous heart.

Laughter and the strumming of a guitar drifted in through the fly of the tent, reminding Genevieve of her surroundings. Picking up her cup of lemon and green tea, she rolled her shoulders, easing the tension in her tired muscles. She walked out of the tent and over to the group, settling into a canvas chair by the fire.

Yellow and orange flames danced against the black velvet night. A light breeze indicated a change of season, but it wasn't quite cool enough for a jacket. Genevieve inhaled the woody scent of smoke and sighed. *This is bliss. Thank you, Jesus.*

It was the last night of the hike through Giraween National Park.

Walking through the granite outcrops interspersed with wildflowers had been challenging, yet exhilarating. Some of the boys had been on previous hikes with David, but there were a few new faces in the mix. Contentment washed over her as she eyed the exuberant faces of the teens and their amazing leader sitting around the fire.

How things had changed in the eighteen months since her release. She couldn't believe this life was really hers. How she had changed from a rebellious woman, who sought love and acceptance in all the wrong places, to someone who was so grateful to be given a second chance. She smiled against her tin cup at the memory of her friend Karina, and thanked God for the way He wound their lives together. Tricia told her God works all things together for good, and she could clearly see that now.

Since joining Elevation Adventures, she'd accompanied David and Brett on overnight hikes, and had also helped Libby and Simon with the day outings. But this was her longest adventure with the group.

The sheer joy on the kids' faces warmed her heart and filled her with pride at David's obedience to God's call on his life. She'd been saddened after hearing some of the stories, but she knew God was working in their lives, just as He'd worked in hers.

"Want a marshmallow, miss?" One of the boys passed her a stick with a toasted marshmallow on the end.

"Thanks." She grinned, removing the warm, sugary snack. Her teeth broke through the crisp outer shell, and she closed her eyes as the warm, gooey centre oozed over her tongue. One sweet snack wouldn't hurt.

Stretching her aching legs out in front of her, she watched as David chatted with two boys on the opposite side of the fire. Bubbles of laughter floated across the flames and one of the boys slapped his thigh in response to something David said.

Smoothing her fingers over the white gold band on her left hand, Genevieve couldn't help but smile. She was beyond blessed. She was not the same woman who stepped foot into the Women's Correctional Centre all those years ago.

She had never known love like the unconditional love she'd received from her friends – Karina, Tom, Tricia, and of course, her husband, David.

Genevieve Molineaux had a nice ring to it. She had hoped her parents would attend the wedding held in New Farm Park six months ago. Instead, her mother had sent her a card, apologizing for not being able to attend, and wishing both her and David well for the future. It wasn't much, but it was the start of healing in their relationship.

Tom had walked Genevieve down the grassy aisle scattered with white rose petals, a wonderful memory for both of them. And David and Genevieve sealed their vows against the stunning backdrop of the Brisbane River.

DAVID SQUIRTED SOME INSECT REPELLANT ONTO HIS ARMS. Genevieve smiled as his hands rubbed over his sun-kissed skin, over the ink and scars now visible for all to see. Still conscious of his scars, David had been reluctant to wear short-sleeved shirts in public. They both still struggled with their insecurities, but David was slowly getting used to his bare arms and allowing his story to be used for God's glory.

God was good. Genevieve still found it difficult to comprehend the vastness of God's love for her, but she was no longer held captive by the mistakes of her past. She could clearly see how He was using her poor choices for His glory. Even blessing her with the the new life blossoming in her womb.

Rubbing her hands across her stomach, Genevieve nestled back into the comfort of the chair, hypnotised by the dancing flames and sleepy after two full days of hiking. A contented smile played on her lips as movement fluttered against her fingertips.

The noise of the teens, the strumming of the guitar and the crackling fire all faded away as David's eyes met hers across the flames, pulling her into an unspoken dance of love and promise.

God had transformed her heart, giving her new life in Him. She knew He wasn't finished with her yet, but she was ready and willing to listen to His call on her life.

Dear Reader,

Thank you for allowing me to share Genevieve's and David's journeys with you. **Heart Transformed** was inspired by an old high school friend whom I ran into at my local church many years after graduating. During high school, and for several years afterwards, he was heavily influenced by drugs, and subsequently made some poor life decisions. When we ran into each other at church, he had left his old life behind, and was working with a charity organisation, helping teens through their recovery from drugs and alcohol. His life was a testament to God's transforming power, and it made me so happy to see God use his past to bless others.

God is so good. And no matter how much we think we've messed up, He is in the business of changing lives and transforming hearts through the redemptive power of His son Jesus. There is nothing too big for Him.

I pray that you will be blessed by this story. You'll find further inspiration and encouragement on The Potter's House Books website, and by reading the other books in this uplifting series. Find all the books on Amazon and on The Potter's House Books website.

Book 1: The Homecoming by Juliette Duncan
Book 2: When it Rains by T.K. Chapin
Book 3: Heart Unbroken by Alexa Verde
Book 4: Long Way Home by Brenda S. Anderson
Book 5: Promises Renewed by Mary Manners
Book 6: A Vow Redeemed by Kristen M. Fraser
Book 7: Restoring Faith by Marion Ueckermann
Book 8: Unchained by Juliette Duncan
Book 9: Gracefully Broken by T.K. Chapin
Book 10: Heart Healed by Alexa Verde
Book 11: Place Called Home by Brenda S. Anderson
Book 12: Tragedy & Trust by Mary Manners
Book 13: Heart Transformed by Kristen M. Fraser
Books 14-12 to be advised

Be notified of all of Kristen's new releases by subscribing to her reader's list (http://www.kristenmfraser.com/newsletter-sign-up.html). You will also receive - **_Lines of Promise_** - free, for signing up.

Enjoyed **_Heart Transformed_**? You can make a big difference...

Help other people find this book by writing a review and telling them why you liked it. Honest reviews of my books help bring them to the attention of other readers just like yourself, and I'd be very grateful if you could spare a few minutes to leave a review (it can be as short as you like) on the book's Amazon page (https:www.amazon.com/dp/B07HLK5DJP).

Blessings,

Kristen.

ABOUT THE AUTHOR

Kristen M. Fraser is a Christian fiction author, residing in beautiful Queensland, Australia with her husband and four children. She drinks way too much coffee, has a far too messy house, and probably doesn't get enough sleep.

Aside from that, Kristen loves worshipping her Creator, running, spending time at the beach, and given a moment of solitude, curling up with a good book.

Although her books are works of fiction, Kristen believes everyone has a story to tell. As such, she takes inspiration for her writing from people's everyday lives - their struggles and successes.

It is her prayer that you will be encouraged and inspired by her words.

Connect with Kristen:
Facebook: https://www.facebook.com/kmfraserauthor
Website: www.kristenmfraser.com
Email: kristenmfraser@outlook.com

Journey to Australia and meet the Harper's in **The Tallowood Valley Series**. Share in the love, loss and hope of this family drama set in rural Australia.

Heart on the Land
(Book 1 - The Tallowood Valley Series)
Chapter One.

1985, country New South Wales, Australia.

Perspiration trickled down Max's back and pooled at the base of his spine as he shifted against the leather seat. Wearing shorts would've been the smarter choice, but coming straight into town after herding the lower paddock and shifting bales between the sheds meant he hadn't had a chance to change out of his work clothes. Another fifteen minutes of waiting and he would be drenched. Summer in Tallowood Valley had well and truly arrived.

Max swatted away the flies buzzing incessantly around his face. Tilting the bran-coloured Akubra over his eyes, he leaned his arm on the window of his dust-covered truck and angled his face towards the hot air flowing through the cab, hoping for a cool breeze to miraculously soothe his sweat-covered face.

"Max! Oi!"

Max raised his hand in greeting as Daniel Hunter jogged across the quiet street adjacent to the railway station.

"What are you doing here?" Daniel rested one arm on top of the truck and leaned down into the window. He glanced at his watch. "I didn't expect to see you in town at this time of day."

Max nodded towards the railway station. "I'm waiting to pick up our new hand."

"Oh, that's right. Your dad mentioned that." Daniel drummed his fingers on the roof of the truck and glanced down the street.

"Yeah, we've been needing a new one for a while after Toby left. Dad's struggling after his hip replacement, and we're getting into the busy season for the stock." The Harper's wheat and cattle property was renowned throughout the region for producing good quality stock. As the only son of Reginald and Patricia Harper, Max was second-in-charge to his father in running Winverall Station, a twenty-minute drive out of town.

"I hope it all goes well, mate. Looks like the train's almost here." Daniel nodded towards the railway station. "Good luck."

"Thanks, Dan," Max replied, taking the keys out of the ignition.

"Stay here, boy." He patted the blue heeler cattle dog panting in the back of the truck.

Adjusting his Akubra, Max took the wooden steps up to the railway station in a few strides. The platform was empty, aside from the station master seated at the ticket booth.

Dust swirled up from the tracks as the incoming train rolled to a stop. An elderly couple and one of the young farmhands from a nearby property were the first passengers to disembark. Max tipped his hat in recognition and strolled along the platform. A young blonde woman lugging a suitcase, and a few other locals stepped off. The doors closed, and the train gave a blast before slowly leaving the station.

With a frown, Max glanced at his watch. 3pm. He was certain he was on time. Perhaps he'd gotten the date wrong. Fumbling with some coins in his pocket, he darted a quick glance along the platform before walking back towards his truck.

"Excuse me." A molten honey voice snagged his attention. Vivid green eyes connected with his as he turned around. Straight, endless blonde hair reflected the afternoon sun, almost blinding him. A blue floral sundress floated around the woman's slender calves, and wedge sandals strapped on her feet brought her level with Max's shoulders. Max swallowed hard, raising an eyebrow as he assessed the woman looking completely out of place on the small town's railway platform.

A small frown creased her brow as she glanced down at a scrap of paper in her hand. "I'm supposed to be meeting someone from Winverall Station."

Max hesitated at her words. "I'm from there."

"Oh, great!" A wide smile lit up her face. "I didn't think I'd ever get here. Tallowood Valley is a long way from Sydney!"

"It sure is." Max nodded, trying to hide his surprise and confusion. "And you are...?"

"Oh! I'm sorry!" The blonde placed her suitcase on the ground and held out her perfectly manicured hand. "Joanna Greaves. Jo for short."

"Jo? Joanna? Jo?" Max stammered as he enclosed her petite hand in his own callused one.

"Yes, that's me. One and the same." She giggled as she swished the skirt of her dress.

"You're kidding." Max chuckled and shook his head as recognition dawned.

Jo snatched her hand back, smoothing down the front of her dress. "What's so funny?"

"Nothing." Max shook his head and ran a hand over his face. "Nothing at all. I just wasn't expecting..." He gestured towards her.

"What?" Jo narrowed her eyes and placed both hands on her hips. "What weren't you expecting?"

"A girl. Well, a woman, to be honest." Max tucked his hands into the back pockets of his dark blue jeans and swallowed the laughter in his throat. *She's got spark. I'll give her credit for that.*

A blush crept up Jo's neck under Max's scrutiny. Frowning, she tilted her head and thrust her chin into the air. "And what's wrong with a woman?" she demanded.

"Nothing. Absolutely nothing." Max's face warmed under the harsh glare of the feisty young woman before him. "When they said 'Jo', I assumed a bloke, that's all." A sheepish grin broke out on his face.

"Well, I'm not a bloke, and you're stuck with me," Jo retorted, folding her arms. "Now, we can stand here all day and debate my name, or you can help me with my luggage and take me somewhere a lot cooler!"

Max dipped his head to hide the smirk twitching at the corner of his mouth, before picking up Jo's brown leather suitcase. He set off down the platform with her wedges clomping along behind him.

Unbelievable. A girl farmhand. A city-slicker Jillaroo. Well, she's in for a big surprise!

Heart on the Land - available now.